C000019121

WAYWARD SOULS

SOULS OF THE ROAD - 1

DEVON MONK

ODD
HOUSE
PRESS

Wayward Souls

Copyright © 2020 by Devon Monk

ISBN: 9781939853219

Publisher: Odd House Press

Cover Art: Ravven

Interior Design: Odd House Press

All rights reserved.

No part of this book may be reproduced in any form or by any electronic or mechanical means, including information storage and retrieval systems, without written permission from the author, except for the use of brief quotations in critical articles or book reviews.

This story is a work of fiction. Names, characters, places, and incidents are the product of the author's imagination or are used fictitiously, and any resemblance to actual persons, living or dead, business establishments, events or locales, is entirely coincidental.

To my family, and all the road-trip dreamers

"There is no one on the road," I said.
"That's what everyone on the road says," he replied.
—Gay Parita Sinclair Station 2018

ACKNOWLEDGMENTS

So many wonderful people helped me bring this book into the world. My greatest gratitude goes out to the ridiculously talented artist, Ravven. Thank you for creating an amazing cover with just the right amount of dusty road, soft magic, and lonely sky.

Huge thank you to my brilliant copy editor, Sharon Elaine Thompson, for once again slaying those pesky grammar gremlins.

To my amazing first reader, Dejsha Knight who read this in its roughest draft. Thank you for seeing what it could be and telling me it was worth it.

Thank you, thank you to the fabulous Eileen Hicks for catching the errors I always seem to miss.

To my sons, Kameron and Konner, I love you both so much. Thank you for being the best part of my life, and letting me be a part of yours. Kam–extra thanks for reminding me this is a "road" book, no matter what else it might be.

To my husband, Russ. Thank you for dropping everything to go off on a wild, wanderlust adventure with me to drive the old Route 66. This book was just a spark of an idea at the time, but traveling that road with you–getting lost, getting found, getting lost again–was one of the most wonderful adventures of my life. Thank you for making all of our adventures wonderful. I love you, always.

To the Travelin' Rats, you keep me dreaming. I can't wait to see what trouble we get into next!

And thank you, dear readers, for coming on this journey with these characters. I hope you enjoyed the trip, and will come back to visit Brogan and Lu soon. Who knows where the road will take them next?

Until we meet again, safe travels, my friends.

CHAPTER ONE

ILLINOIS

Lu wanted the truck.

"It's too old," I repeated.

There were two things going against me winning this argument. One: I was dead, so she couldn't hear me, and two: I was her husband, so she probably wouldn't listen to me anyway.

"I like it." She ran a palm along the hood as if she could tell its life story through touch alone. With her abilities, I wouldn't put it past her. Touching things and knowing their value was likely the only good she'd gotten out of the day we'd died.

Her wedding ring, worn down to a thin gold band, winked dully in the afternoon light and caught like a sharp hook in my heart. I'd told her she could take it off. Told her she should let me go.

I hadn't won that argument either, and didn't I love her all the more for it?

"What do you think, Lorde?" she asked.

"That dog couldn't spot a bad front-end alignment if she were chewing on the axle," I groused.

The dog in question tipped her big, fuzzy black head. She was part chow chow, and part shepherd. From the way her eyes tracked me, as I leaned against the back bumper of the truck, I knew at least one of my girls was listening.

I bent forward so my face was closer to the dog. "Tell her Brogan says it has a bad radiator, it's leaking oil, and the electrical is shot."

Lorde panted, her black tongue almost disappearing against all that black fur. She barked once.

"Atta girl," I said. "Front. End. Alignment."

She dutifully barked three times.

"Okay, okay," Lu said. "I get it. You like the truck too."

The dog wagged her tail. I groaned.

Lu plucked the weathered FOR SALE sign off the cracked windshield and marched toward the crooked front stoop of the house, determination in every lean line of her.

"That was a no!" I threw my arms up and stared at the wide blue arc of Illinois sky.

"You're gonna spend twice as much time under that thing as in it," I said. "Lu. Lula, just…touch the watch. Listen to me. Talk to me." I strode up to the house with her, an easy lope. Moving as a spirit through the world meant the world had very little impact upon me, and I didn't have much on it either.

Unless I got angry.

Then I could tear this world to shreds.

But this wasn't something that needed my anger.

A frown put three lines between her auburn eyebrows. Her wide mouth tightened at the corners like she was half chewed through a lemon. That, along with the look of resolve in her eyes, just made me love her more.

She was being a bit of a sap about the truck, but that didn't stop me from wanting to pull her in my arms and kiss the hell out of her.

"Listen." I put a little more energy behind the command this time.

Lu paused, one foot on the rickety first step. Her hand lifted toward the heavy gold pocket watch hung on a thick chain around her neck. She didn't touch it. Not yet.

She was beautiful, my Lu. Cherry hair wild around a pale face that freckled good and hard but never tanned, even before, when she was much more alive, and much more human.

Now she was a *thrawan*—that step between being almost killed by a vampire, but not turning out to be either of those things: killed or a vampire. I supposed she'd scan as human in any of those computerized machines the world used for medicine now.

The only outward hint that she was something else, something *other*, was that she was incredibly strong, sensitive to magic, and lonelier than anyone deserved to be.

The loneliness was my fault too.

Somehow, a shred of my soul beat fiercely inside her, just as a slip of her soul had stuck deep in me.

Neither of us knew how we'd traded pieces of our souls. It might have been during the attack, as I lay dying, watching the monster feed on her.

Our gazes had locked and then…

…then everything had gone black. It was a good blackness. Peaceful, warm.

Until I'd woke into the shattering of her scream.

She: bent over my unbreathing, unresponsive body.

Me: standing above myself—poor dead bastard—unable to close the deal, finish the story.

There was no white light guiding me up, no red flames dragging me down. I wouldn't have wanted them anyway. All I wanted was her.

I was more dead than alive, she was more alive than dead, and as far as we could tell, we were stuck that way.

After ninety years, we'd both given up on the why and had moved solidly onto the how.

As in: how could we kill the assholes who did this to us?

Back when we were alive—the Dirty Thirties, they called it—monsters had been on the move.

Boats, trains, roads, highways did as much to move the supernatural critters across the country and around the world as it had the humans.

People settled down to make homes, businesses, towns. Monsters staked out their territories, claimed their towns, cities, and hidden patches of land.

The monsters were still out there, still here, all around us. Moving as much as they liked, or staying put and setting down roots.

And it wasn't just monsters who moved through the

modern world. The gods were among us, meddling in the lives of mortals for reasons of their own. I'd even heard there was some sort of town out in Oregon where the gods liked to vacation.

"Touch the watch," I urged Lu. "Ask me if I like the truck. We agreed all big purchases have to have both our approval. Remember that accordion? Or the beehives? Or that boat? Ask me, sweetheart."

I stood in front of her and hooked my thumbs in my belt.

"'Cause those tires ain't looking too good either." I pushed need and desire toward her, focusing hard. It was a fifty-fifty chance she'd sense me, much less hear me, but it didn't stop me from trying.

"You like trucks," she whispered, her eyes skipping right past me to focus on the wilted patch of thistles leaning against the porch. "I like the truck. I can modify the back. Put in a bed, a light. Some of your books."

Sorrow squeezed what was left of my heart. I reached for her, unable to stop, my fingers brushing along the side of her face, down her shoulder, her arm to rest on her wrist.

Her honey-colored eyes went wide and distant. She shivered before closing them.

"Plus silver's your favorite color," she whispered.

"Ah, love." I wanted to kiss her, wanted to feel her, warm and soft and tender in my arms. But she was mist, only the slightest sensation of warmth on my fingertips, like a dream half forgotten and fading in daylight.

"Lorde and I are going to dicker the owner down by half." She held up the sign like maybe I hadn't noticed her plucking it off the truck. As if I'd miss a single thing she did. "If not, we walk." She opened her eyes, waited for me to say something else, then marched up the stairs.

I chuckled at the stubborn set of her shoulders. Whoever lived in that house didn't know what was about to hit them. "All right. All right. Give 'em hell, girl."

CHAPTER TWO

I t was a big silver lug of a thing, sporting the newest technology of its time: an AM radio and a push-in cigarette lighter.

It had exactly six hundred sixty six miles on it.

Lu took it as a sign.

I took it as a sign the guy knew how to reset the odometer and might be into that show about Satan.

But the seats were buttery soft black vinyl, the windows cranked up and down by hand, and the bed in back was wood and not lined with that stuff that could withstand an atom bomb.

I sprawled on the passenger side of the big bench seat as she cruised down the narrow road, her window yawning wide so one hand could swim in the warm air as it rushed past.

We'd left Chicago behind us, following the road past tall buildings and crowded sidewalks, then into neighborhoods with cracked pavement, old parks and older churches, until we'd threaded out into Cicero. Lu hadn't stopped at Henry's Drive-in for a hot dog. She hadn't stopped in Lyons or McCook or Romeoville. When we rolled past the Rich and Creamy ice cream stand with JOLIET KICKS ON 66 written across a giant ice cream cone set behind two life-size statues of the Blues Brothers dancing on the roof, I figured Lu wasn't gonna stop driving all day.

She was focused, but easy, letting the road spool out behind us like there was something out there calling her name and all she had to do was follow it.

Illinois spread around us, flat and wide. The sun caught yellow in the deep green of cornfields and tall grasses, the sky arched in powder blue above scattered oak and maple trees. Lorde panted like a fuzzy sentinel between us, staring out the open window on my side, but not crowding me out of my seat to get to it.

I nodded at the Gemini Giant in Wilmington, the thirty-foot tall statue of a man in green coveralls and space helmet, still grinning about the silver rocket in his hands after all these years. Then I watched as Braidwood, Godley, and Gardner came and went.

Lu stopped at the Ambler's Texaco Service Station to let Lorde out onto the grassy area to do her business. The little white cottage with the green roof had been built in 1933, and pumped gas for the next sixty-six years or so. It had fallen into disrepair for some years before it was restored as a visitor's center.

Didn't look like anyone but us had visited for awhile.

I leaned against the fire engine red Texaco Sky Chief gas pumps and tipped my head to get the kink out of my neck. The billboard behind the picnic tables declared: MY FAMILY'S DESTINATION IS DWIGHT ILLINOIS. I wondered if the unimpressed man in the fedora on the sign was supposed to be Frank Sinatra.

After that, a steady row of small towns rose up and grew small as we continued on: Odell, Cayuga, Pontiac, Lexington.

"Don't name it Silver," I finally said after we'd passed through the old growth hickory, oak, and maple trees of Funks Grove, leaving the MAPLE SIRUP sign—spelled just that way—behind. We were mid-way through the route in Illinois, and Lu was still driving.

"How about Silver? That's a good name." Lu reached out and scratched behind one of Lorde's kitten-soft ears.

I grunted. "You've already named a snail, a cow, and a Studebaker Silver."

"Silver's good. The Lone Ranger's horse was Silver, and he was strong and reliable. Just like you." She patted the dash.

The truck coughed, shuddered, and made a grossly exaggerated popping sound.

"No, no, no," she breathed, fighting the wheel as she lost speed.

"How about Anchor?" I suggested, watching the dials bottom out and stay there. "Scrap Metal? Shipwreck? I mean, Bad Decision might be a bit on the nose, but it could work."

The truck lurched, howled at the injustices of life, then banged like a sawed-off shotgun before coming to a dead stop.

She blinked a couple times while the dust kicked up from the road did a slow roll through the cab, leaving behind a layer of brown.

"Or, you know, you could call it the I Told You So," I said.

"Damn-to-hell. If you are laughing at me, Brogan, so help me, I'll make you pay."

I grinned and leaned her way waggling my eyebrows even though she couldn't see me. "Oh, big words. How you gonna make me any worse off than I already am, darlin'?"

She thunked her head back on the bench and blew out a big breath. "It was just a few more miles."

"To the junkyard, where this thing belongs?" I asked.

"We're closer to McLean than Shirley, aren't we?" she muttered.

"Yes."

"Walk or call?" she asked Lorde.

"Call a tow," I said. "Lorde. Tell her to call a tow."

Lorde's ears tipped back, then forward. The road dust had painted her black coat grizzly bear brown. She hopped down to the floorboards, and scooched past my legs to stick her head out the window. Nothing but farmland beyond the railroad tracks on our right and more farmland beyond I-55 on our left.

The air in the cab was warm enough even I could feel it, maybe somewhere in the high nineties Fahrenheit, which was no surprise since it was July in Illinois.

I guess one of the only good things about not being

alive was that humidity wasn't much of a bother. It was a dry death.

"Too hot to walk with all that black fur," Lu said. "Let's see what I can find."

She reached across me, stretching for the glove box. I inhaled out of habit, wishing I could catch the deep rose and honey scent of her perfume.

The glove box popped, and she dug out the cellular phone she'd dropped in there just a couple hours ago.

For all that the world didn't seem to notice my existence, and I couldn't smell it or touch it like a living man should, everything else about me felt a lot like what living had been like. Or at least what I remembered.

I certainly had my share of fatigue, hunger, and stiff muscles from too much sitting.

But I didn't need to open the door to exit the truck. It was easier to just drift through it.

Lorde shifted out of my way so I could ease out of the cab to stretch my legs.

I'd only drifted through living things a handful of times when I was first trying to get the hang of Unliving. It was not an experience I enjoyed, and Lorde seemed to know that.

I gave her a pat on the head, then did a once-around the truck. The sky still blue as a bachelor button, not even a lint's worth of cloud from horizon to horizon. The sound of faster vehicles, modern vehicles, hushed and growled and huffed down the freeway.

An entire modern world that Lu and I had discovered was a no-man's land for us.

Stepping too far off the Route didn't do either of us

any good. Because it wasn't just our souls we'd snipped and traded. Somehow that old road had a say in just how alive we could be.

Close to Route 66 was good. On the Route was best. Getting too far off it, stretching out into the modern world, was bad.

The Route threaded us together, stitched us to this world with an asphalt needle. Neither of us knew why, we just knew it was true.

I leaned against the bumper again and tipped my face up, imagining I could feel that sunlight on my skin, in my muscles, feel it soaking down to my cold, cold bones.

The truck dipped and Lu stepped out. "Yeah, just north of McLean, below Funks Grove on Route 66. If you hit Shirley, you went too far. It's a big ol' silver Chevy. You can't miss it. Yeah. Okay. Good."

She pocketed the phone in those tight jeans she wore because she knew it drove me wild to see her in denim. "Come on, Lorde, let's stretch our legs." She snapped her fingers and Lorde jumped down out of the truck, her black tongue already lolling. She glanced at Lu, glanced back at me.

I made with the shooing motions. "Get your walk in. No telling how long it will be until they send a tow truck. I'll come get you when they arrive."

Lorde sniffed at me, sneezed, then shook her head and trotted over to Lu. Lu had been doing this long enough to know I was near the truck.

She held up one hand in a wave, even though her eyes were focused over my shoulder.

I held a couple of fingers up to her, watched her turn and walk down the road with her hand resting on Lorde's head. The way she filled out those jeans, Wranglers should pay that woman for carrying their label over her back pocket.

She must have felt me watching her, 'cause she paused and gave her hips a little extra wiggle before striding off. I chuckled, closed my eyes, and went back to wishing for sunlight.

CHAPTER THREE

L u had found a water bottle in her knapsack and was sipping from it. She sat cross-legged on the hood of the hunk of junk, her sunglasses on, but not a hat. Sunlight was hard for her in quantity, but a few hours out in it wouldn't do her any harm.

I knew she was tracking the tow truck long before it was in sight, knew she could tell how many people were in it by the heartbeat—one man—and that he was in his early thirties, in good health.

I could tell all that stuff, too, because I'd drifted over to the oncoming truck and had taken a look with my own eyes.

When the driver pulled through a neat turn to back the tow to the front end of poor broken down Silver— which was never gonna be its name—I knew something about the man interested her. It was in the tip of her head, in the elevated speed of her breathing, in the pause between swallows as she watched him through narrowed eyes.

And if Lu was interested in a human being, then so was I.

"Lorde," Lu called. "Lorde."

The dog immediately trotted over from whatever she was sniffing at the side of the road. The driver killed the engine and dropped down with that easy grace of youth, like time hadn't found a way to crack his shell and take bites out of the vital parts of him yet.

If sunlight could walk around in a pair of tan Dickies and a short-sleeve, button-up shop shirt with CALVIN stitched in blue embroidery over the pocket, then this is what it would look like.

More than just straw-colored hair, bangs of which would be in his eyes if they weren't finger-combed back, he had smooth, clean skin gone golden tan and blue eyes that gave the sky a run for its money.

He moved, every step warm sunshine and easy roads. There was something more in his smile. Something white and bright and clean and good.

I immediately didn't like the guy. Too tall, too blond, too good looking.

"Afternoon," he said, flashing the smile. "Everything okay? I heard you praying? Calling for the Lord?"

"I wasn't praying." Lu pointed down at our dog. "The Lorde is my shepherd."

Sunshine paused, then he cackled. "Oh, that's good. Really good. Lorde. Clever."

"Give it a break, Sunshine," I muttered. "She's got

decades of chewing up and spitting out pretty boys like you."

Lorde, sitting so close to me by the front bumper she'd be leaning on my leg if I were solid, got to her feet and cut Sunshine off before he was close enough to extend a hand to Lu.

"Hey, there," the guy said. "Lorde. Aren't you a beauty?" He dropped his hand, let Lorde give it a sniff and stood still, watching as she circled him, sniffing his boots, pants, and anything else in her reach.

By the time she got around to the front of him again, her tail was slowly wagging and her black tongue was out. He reached down and scratched between her fuzzy black ears. "She part Akita?"

"Chow chow, German shepherd," Lu said. There was caution in her voice, but there was also a lot of curiosity. Uh-oh. Lu's curiosity got the both of us into more trouble than you could carry in a bucket. "You're Calvin?"

"Yes, Ma'am. Calvin Fisher. Fisher's Auto is my shop. You called in and talked to Ray. That is if you called for a tow?"

Lu tipped her sunglasses down so she could see over the top of them.

I leaned back on one elbow to watch his reaction.

"I hear ya, buddy," I said, "those eyes, right? You want to fall all the way in and drink until you drown. 'Course the red hair ain't doing her no damage."

I pushed away from the front bumper to stand to one side of where Lu was still sitting on the hood and watch him try not to swallow his tongue.

"I did." Lu held her hand out. "Lu," she offered. "Lu Gauge."

He took her hand, and if her skin was cooler than any person sitting on a truck hood baking in the sun in the middle of Illinois had the right to be, he didn't say anything.

"Pleasure," he said. "So I can take you up to Bloomington or down to Lincoln. Happy to get you out to your place if you're staying in the area?"

"What makes you think I'm just driving through?"

He smiled, pouring on the charm, and it popped a dimple in one cheek.

"Oh, give me a break. You're human, right?" I circled him just like the dog had before me, looking for any marks or signs that he was something supernatural. Maybe a siren or a god pretending to be human, or one of those gorgeous, dangerous Faefolk.

Nothing.

"Most people take the highway," he said. "People on the Route are on it for the road itself. Getting their kicks on Route 66. That, or they're locals who know the back roads. You aren't local. I'd remember you if you lived around here."

"That right?" she asked. The woman was not flirting. She hadn't even smiled yet. But Lu usually ignored people any chance she got. Seeing her chatting it up with the boy was irritating. And interesting.

"What do you see in him, Lu? You like that look?" I tipped my head to do some calculations on if he was her type.

He was my opposite, that was for sure. If he was

sunlight, I was the night sky. Dark hair, pale skin, eyes the color of stones. I'd been told by more than one woman that I was dangerously handsome, and maybe that was true.

But this man didn't have any of my hard edges, didn't have my build—I was a good four inches taller than him, and he had to be a six-footer if he was an inch. And while he had a good strong build—shoulders hard from working, stomach flat, good muscles in his arms—I could bench press him with one hand tied behind my back.

What I'm saying is I'm a big man. Broad at the shoulder, thick at the hip, but not fat. Not even in life and certainly not in death.

"You'd remember if I lived around here?" she repeated.

"Sure," Sunshine drawled. "Truck like this isn't something you see every day."

There was a beat, a pause where Lu and I both took a minute just to stare at him.

He could have gone for the cheesy line, the pick-up line, told her she had skin like snow and hair like fire. But instead he'd made a crack about the crappy truck.

"Nope," I said. "Still don't like you, Sunshine."

But then something pretty damn rare happened. Lu smiled at him.

I groaned. Whatever caught her interest wasn't gonna stop here.

"Just picked it up," Lu said. "Thought I'd get to a shop somewhere along the way and have him checked out. Looks like it's all going to plan."

Sunshine chuckled and ran fingers back through those too-long bangs. "Well, then. Let me know where you'd like me to take him, and we'll get you all set."

"Fisher Auto come recommended?" she asked.

He nodded. "It's been said it's the nicest little shop this side of the Mississippi."

Lu raised an eyebrow.

"Well, my mom said it, so there might be some bias there."

"I Googled you."

"Ah. Well, then."

"Not a single bad review."

"I'm sure I'll get one eventually. Can't please everyone."

"No, you can't." Lu dropped down off of the hood, her boots planting in the dust and gravel. "But then, not everybody deserves to be pleased. I'll get my stuff."

"Fisher's?" he asked.

"Fisher's."

CHAPTER FOUR

W e'd been in every town dug down or sprung up along the Route. We'd seen them rise up slowly like a planted crop, seen them thrive and spread, or falter and crumble down to dust under the hammer of the years.

The big business keeping McLean on the map was the Dixie Truck Stop and café. Built back in 1928, the place had survived storms and disaster and only missed one day serving food and fuel. That was because the place burned down and had to be temporarily located to a nearby house while rebuilding.

It'd changed hands from family ownership some time back, but the restaurant was still standing right in the middle of a big, wide, flat stretch of pavement with room for dozens of trucks. Route 66 and I-55 ran north/south on either side, the truck stop its own island in between.

Directly across from the parking lot stood a little

green train depot—one of the two left that had seen Abraham Lincoln's funeral car rumble past—unremarkable except for a sign marking it as an important place.

Someone had set up a model train store in it. I thought that wasn't such a bad thing.

Fisher's Auto, however, wasn't anywhere near the truck stop. It was on the north side of town, right at the fork in the road between Fisher Street and Route 66. From the look of the place, it was once a home with a barn, and now the barn was an auto shop, which was, much as Mother Fisher had remarked, nice.

The streets were concrete, cracked from hard summers and harder winters, grass growing up in the middle of it wherever it caught root.

A couple kids on bikes churned past, none of them old enough to be teens, and none of them worried about rambling around town on their own.

Sunshine made quick work of backing the old truck into the garage space then glanced over at Lu. "We can take care of the paperwork inside. You're welcome to stay or maybe get a cup of coffee or lunch—we have a good diner just down around the block a bit. I'll give you a call with a quote before we start in on repairs. How's that sound?"

"Like we aren't getting out of Illinois tonight," I said from where I'd crammed myself behind the seats, my shoulders tipped at an angle that stuck them square in the middle of the seat ahead of me, but kept them out of actually pressing into Lu.

Walking through a living person was hard. Pressing into Lu was an ache I'd only tried once.

It'd left us both so shaken and wanting, I'd vowed I'd never do it again. Ghost possession was not an easy ride.

Lou reached for the door handle. "Any rooms open around here?"

I raised my eyebrows. Lu didn't sleep much. But when she did it was always under the stars, or better yet, in a graveyard where we had a better chance of really being together. Of hearing each other.

Hotels were a mess of old pain, ghosts, monsters, and less desirable things.

It wasn't just humans who lived in these parts, after all.

"We've got the Super 8 just outside of town. Water's hot. Clean sheets." He dropped out of the truck, following her and Lorde. I exhaled and drifted through the cab of the truck, then out through the door.

I stomped my feet to get some feeling back into them. It was a true injustice that even as an almost dead-guy, cramped quarters still made my feet tingly.

"Something quieter?" Lu asked.

Sunshine hummed, thinking about it. He quickly stepped in front of her and opened the door to the building before she got there.

"I'd offer you my shop WiFi to do a little searching, but my wireless is out. The crap wireless company hasn't sent me another crap repair guy since the last crap repair guy was here twiddling his crap thumbs."

Lu listened to him—Lu always listened. But she wasn't looking at him. She was taking the measure of the woman who stood just inside the open door.

The woman had golden brown skin and glossy black

hair that was tight-shaved on one side of her head but long on the other. Tiny gold rings sparkled in her dark eyebrow, ears, and nose, and her brown eyes were lined with black pencil that did that little wing thing at each corner.

More jewelry—silver, hemp, bead, leather— wrapped the wrist that was resting on a messenger bag slung over her shoulder. Shirt was white and pants were black, and that messenger bag had a logo on it that said: QUALITY CABLE AND COMPUTER REPAIR.

"Oh, Sunshine. You are so screwed." I laughed and rubbed my hands together. This was gonna be good.

Sunshine followed Lu's gaze and noticed the woman standing in the shop. "Can I help you?"

"Sure," she said. "I'm your crap repair guy here to do crap nothing while I twiddle these crappers." She held up her thumbs and delivered a glare that looked like it was gonna be followed by a kick in the nads.

Sunshine made a weird croaking sound, cleared his throat, and coughed.

She just kept right on glaring.

He went beet red and wrapped one hand around the back of his neck. "I…uh. Okay. I'll show you to the… uh…wireless. Junction. Router. And the computer that's not working." He gestured for Lu to precede him into the building.

Lu looked at Sunshine, looked at Quality, and then she got this gleam in her eyes.

"No," I said. "No, nope, no. You are not going to hook this joker up with the brainy computer gal."

Lu rubbed her thumb along the side of her pointer finger like she was consulting an oracle stone.

"Do not play Cupid. Lu. You have no right to meddle in people's lives. Just move on. Get the truck fixed. I don't think Sunshine over here is good enough for Quality, no matter how many dimples he has."

"Lu," she said, sticking her hand out toward the woman and stepping into the building.

The room was too small to be a lobby, but obviously served as one. Repair bays were beyond the door marked as such to the left, a hallway stretched straight ahead, and it looked like an office was about mid-way on the right.

"Jo," Quality replied, shaking firmly.

Sunshine couldn't keep his big stupid shoes out of his big, stupid mouth.

"Jo? Is that short for Josephine or something?"

She raised one eyebrow. "It's just Jo."

I grinned. "Atta girl. Don't give an inch. It's a good name."

"Nice name," Lu said.

I groaned. When she was picking—antique hunting for the dealer who paid top dollar for her to find rare and usually magical items—she was all about chatting up a seller. But out among normal life and normal folk, my Lu didn't like to rub more than two words together.

Picking kept money in the bank. It also gave us a chance to dig for artifacts and magical items that might bring us closer to solving our Unliving problem.

It was a thin hope, one that had gotten thinner over the years. But if there was a chance we might be able to change what happened to us, we weren't going to give up on it.

Lu sure as hell wasn't going to back down. And if we couldn't fix the almost-dead of our existence, well, then between the two of us, we still had more than enough anger to hunt down the bastards who did this to us.

"Don't get in the middle of this oil jockey's business, Lu," I went on. "Why are you trying to shine him up anyway? That apple ain't worth Jo's time."

"My parents liked it," Jo replied.

Lu nodded like that was plenty good enough reason. "They local?"

"Texas."

"Nice out there," Lu said.

"Can be."

During all this, Sunshine stood there, silent, looking like he'd rather be anywhere else than in the middle of the small talk.

"You been to Texas?" Lu asked Calvin, reeling him on in.

"Here we go," I muttered. "I am going to bet you— right here and right now—that you will regret playing Cupid. Again. It never works out, Lu."

Sunshine let out a hard breath. "No. Never wanted too. Never got along much with those people."

"Well, that's real nice," I said. "Disrespecting on a woman's hometown."

"And you're still batting a thousand with *those people*," Jo said.

Lu raised her auburn eyebrows like she couldn't believe Sunshine had let that fall outta his mouth.

Sunshine looked disappointed in himself too. He was back to that root vegetable color, his jaw locked. "Yeah. Yes. Sorry. So, um, let's get you to the office. That is if you still want to take the job after I've been… well…" He rubbed his hand over the back of his neck again.

Quality looked like she wanted to say no, but she nodded. "That's what I'm here for. Office this way?"

"Yes, here, let me." Sunshine angled his body past the two women and made short work of crossing the little lobby and opening the office door.

The office was slightly larger than the lobby. Shelves stacked with papers and manuals lined the walls, a small red refrigerator sat in one corner. A desk with what I assumed was the wireless router and a computer that even I knew was out of style took up most the space.

Lu waited in the little lobby, but I knew she'd hear every word.

I followed Jo, who paused in the office doorway, then reached for her messenger bag strap, pulling it up and over her head.

"So the wireless just, uh…stopped working about two weeks back," Sunshine said. "It would connect at first, but every time it did, the printer kicked in and started printing out garbage. Couldn't get it to stop. And when I finally unplugged the internet box, it wouldn't turn back on. Neither would the printer or the computer."

"Where have you been doing your printing?" I wondered as Jo pulled back the rolling chair. It was old enough to have come original with the shop, but it was in good shape—no tears in the dark brown leather, no creaking in the wheels.

"I've been doing my printing over at the diner. Owner knows me."

I smiled and shook my head. That happened sometimes. I asked a question and somehow a Living heard me and answered.

"They have Wi-Fi too. I'd be happy to have lunch brought over for you. On me," he added.

Jo sat, tipped her boots to balance on her toes, like she was ready to dive off into a pool or jump off the starting blocks.

"No thanks." She pressed a button on the computer, bit her bottom lip softly, and narrowed her eyes.

"This password protected?" she asked.

"No. I shut down whenever I'm out of the office, and the doors are locked at night. Don't need more security than that."

She scoffed.

"Small town, Miss…?" he tried.

She flicked a look his way. "Jo."

"Miss Jo," he repeated.

"Just Jo's good enough."

"Sorry about—" He waved in the general direction of the lobby and presumably the conversation they'd had there. "You caught me by surprise. Good surprise," he added real quick. "I didn't mean to disrespect you. Or your business." He winced. "Or your state."

There was a pause, and she wasn't looking at the computer any more. She was looking at him. Really looking.

He smiled, popping dimples, then he dragged his hand through those over-long bangs.

I could hear her heart pick up the pace. Could sense other things too. How her breathing got a little stuttered, how her pupils widened.

"You gonna fall for a pretty face, Jo?" I asked her. "He insulted your company and your hometown. Don't let him get away with that small-town-boy charm."

"I'm going to get to work now, Mr. Fisher." Just like that, whatever moment Sunshine had been trying to construct folded like a bad poker hand.

"Sure. I'll just… I'll be out in the bay if you need me. Or anything. If you need anything. I'll…uh…leave you to it. And lunch. Think about lunch."

He put the skee in the daddle and got out of the office real fast.

He started to close the office door, stopped, opened it like he was going to say something, then shook his head and left it open a crack. Enough Jo had privacy, not so much he couldn't hear her if she called out for him.

"The diner has wireless?" Lu asked, like she'd just happened to overhear that one part of the conversation. Lorde was lying on the floor next to her right where the air conditioner breeze crossed the lobby.

"MaryJo's. Free wireless, coffee as plain or fancy as you like, and everything's cooked from scratch. Need directions?"

"I'll find it."

"All right," he said, throwing a look over his shoulder at the office, then shaking his head slightly before focusing on Lu again. "Enjoy your lunch. I'll have an idea of what's going on with the truck by the time you get back."

Lu raised two fingers in a good-bye, snapped for Lorde to follow, then sauntered out of the shop and into the sun.

CHAPTER FIVE

"That man over there's staring at you," I said to Lu.

She tipped her head, as if she'd heard a faraway voice. I wasn't far away though. I was sitting across from her at the little picnic table set in the shade outside the diner.

Lu took another bite of fries, her sharp white teeth neatly severing the crunchy potato.

"He's been staring at you since you walked out of the shop. He followed you here."

Lu flicked a quick glance over at the man who was sitting in the cab of his truck, windows up, engine running. He appeared to be scrolling through his phone, not watching Lu, but I'd been in that cab just a minute ago to check him out.

He wasn't messing with a phone. He was listening to a talk show saying there was a severe lack of Jesus in these parts. From the cross hanging off his review mirror and the silver one he had tucked under his white, button-down shirt, I thought the radio show was preaching to the choir.

I also thought he was a vampire hunter.

"He's hunting," I said.

Lu made a little humming sound and went back to her fries. She dropped one hand to pet Lorde who was tight up against her, lying under the table.

I shifted forward and stretched across the scarred-up wooden table, pressing my fingertips against the pocket watch she was wearing under her shirt. I focused, really focused.

"Hunter," I said, pushing that word out through my body, my fingers, my soul. Urging the word to reach into that watch, to those moments we still had left to us. Willing that word to reach through it to her, into her, so she would know, so she would hear me even though we were not in a graveyard and the watch was not ticking.

"Hunter, Lu."

She shivered and closed her eyes, inhaling like she'd just caught the scent of flowers, or like she'd just gentled herself down into a warm, soothing bath.

"I know, baby," I said. "I miss you too." I didn't draw my fingers away. She couldn't hear me, but I kept talking. "We'll find a way through this. You and I. But right now, baby, open your eyes. That man doesn't like the look of you. Or maybe likes it too much. You need to get moving."

I pulled back, rocking to sit on the bench, which was almost too small for me. She opened her eyes, blinked and blinked, and for that one, swift moment, she looked vulnerable, sad.

She looked lonely.

Then the hard edges were back. An armor no one could crack. Well, no one but me. And I tried not to. I knew she needed that hard exterior to keep herself together. To keep herself safe.

She had more than just her armor to keep her safe. She had me. I wasn't going to let anything hurt her again.

"That truck right there." I pointed, then cleared the roughness out of my voice. "Might just be a local who's never seen a woman as beautiful as you. Might be a hunter who's trying to decide how much vampire you have in you. Either way, he is not friendly."

Lu popped a couple more fries in her mouth while swinging up off the bench. She offered a small handful to Lorde, who took them gently, then swallowed them down in two quick chomps, wagging her tail.

Lu and Lorde strolled out into the sunshine, taking their time.

The man watched. Waiting to see if her skin steamed.

Vampires weren't killed by sunlight. But it was not comfortable. They usually wore long sleeves, kept their hands in their pockets, and found some way to keep a hat and sunglasses handy.

Lu stopped right there in the parking lot, pulling her phone out like she was looking for directions.

I glanced down at the screen.

"Bed and breakfasts? Around here? You're dreaming, girl."

She swiped her thumb over the screen, and little markers showed up on a map. She tapped on one and read through the listing—it was an Airbnb—then scrolled to the next.

"Still don't know why you want a bed. Gonna be a good night for the stars." I walked away from her, covering the distance to the watcher in the truck. I leaned on the door and stuck my head in through the closed window so I could get a look at him again.

He was still tracking her movements, but something about him had changed. He didn't look like he planned to jump out of the truck and attack her. As a matter of fact, he had another kind of look. One I wouldn't stand for.

"She's taken, buddy," I said. "You get anywhere near her, and I'll knock your head off."

He exhaled and looked back down at his phone.

I drifted back over to Lu.

"I think he's just horny," I said. "But let's not give him a chance to prove me wrong. Lorde?"

Lorde lifted her bear-like face.

"Back to the truck, girl. Head on back. Truck." I pointed in the general direction of Sunshine's shop.

Lorde took a step, then another, and looked back at Lu.

"Oh, is that how it is?" Lu asked Lorde, even though I knew she was asking me. "Just walk away?"

"That's how it is. I don't like that guy, and Sunshine said he'd have news on the truck."

"I think Calvin likes Jo." Lu held her hand out from her side just a bit as she walked. I came up beside her and wove my fingers through hers. I could feel her warmth, but I didn't know if she could feel the cold of me.

Still, we'd had enough years to know where the other person was. Always.

"He's a small town hick who insulted her and told her he hates Texas. I don't like him."

"I like him," she said.

"Lu."

"He reminds me of that man, was it Robert? He worked the docks. Always putting his foot in his mouth when he saw a woman he liked. Awkward as hell. But good I think. I think he's good, Brogan."

I inhaled through my nose and glared in the general direction of the shop. "I think he's too big for his britches."

"And Jo. She's something," Lu said. "I mean, I don't think she's his type."

"What? What's wrong with her? She's aces. Doesn't back down. She'd keep a man on his toes. Who wouldn't like that type of woman?"

"She's too big city for him. Too ready for a fight. Gonna go through the world lonely if all she does is punch first."

"Punching first is good. Punching first keeps you safe," I said. "*You* punch first."

"Maybe I'll stick around and see if I can make this work out for him. For them. If she feels the same kind of way for him I think he might feel for her."

"She doesn't."

"She might," she answered, as if she'd heard me. "She might. As a matter of fact, I'll make you a bet."

"You are not Cupid, Lu."

"I bet you Calvin will be dating Jo before I leave town."

"You don't want to do that. Embarrass yourself like that."

She paused, as if waiting for me to say more.

"Don't be chicken, Brog. Tell me it's a bet. I get Calvin to date Jo, and we name the truck Silver."

"What if you don't get Calvin to date Jo?"

"If you win," she said, "which isn't going to happen, you can name the truck anything you want."

"Like I Told You So? Because it's either that or You Shouldn't Make Bets You Can't Win. Top contenders, hands down."

"Yes. Your pick."

"All right," I said, warming up to the game. "If Sunshine's—Calvin's—dating Jo, which I don't see happening in a million, Silver is the go. But if Jo avoids making poor decisions—such as dating Calvin—then it's the I Told You So all the way."

She nodded. "I thought you'd like that."

"Cupid's a real god, Lu. A dangerous one at that. He's not some little angel with a cute bow and heart-tipped arrows. His arrows are made of gold and lead—what one connects, the other can destroy—and it's not just people he uses them on. He can force heaven and earth, light and darkness, worlds and universes together, or tear them apart. And he's out in the world. You shouldn't meddle in the business of gods."

"I'm gonna find a place to stay—a real bed," she said, ignoring me. "A shower. Maybe take off my boots for a day or two. I know hotels aren't good for you, but there's a nice house renting out a couple rooms just down the street the other way. Let's see how that one feels, okay?"

I sighed. "You don't have to decide where you're staying on my account," I said. "Anywhere there's you, is good with me."

"Anywhere there's you is where I'm gonna be," she said.

I squeezed her hand a little harder, even though she couldn't feel it.

CHAPTER SIX

"It's not much," Mrs. Just-call-me-Dot-Doris-was-my-mother's-name said as she strode through the old, three-story house that had been renovated into rentable rooms. Dot was short, round, and powerful, like she'd been bulling her way through brick walls and glass ceilings all her life. She had on a gauzy kind of bright orange shirt and white pants. Her shoes sparkled with little rhinestones on the sides of them.

I liked her immediately.

"But the mattress is top-of-the-line, and I only use the softest sheets. You'll have a view of the neighborhood, breakfast is available in the kitchen—I bring it in from BunBun Bakery, because a chef I am not—and the bathroom's right down the hall."

She stopped at the door painted a soft green, inserted an old brass key, and gave it a turn before pushing the door open.

"This is it," she said proudly.

I walked into the room before Lu could, shouldering by both woman and trying my best not to touch them. Lorde followed on my heels. The walls were painted white with touches of that soft green on the molding and the edges of the window sills. Everything else in the room was white and green too, with a few pops of blue flowers on the pillows, a lamp, and a lap quilt.

I drifted over to stand by the window and gave the room one last look.

It was clean, bright. A soothing sort of place.

Which was probably why the woman was sitting in the padded chair in the corner, her eyes closed, her knitting pooled in her lap.

Great. A ghost.

I hated ghosts.

"Lorde. Tell Lu we have company." I pointed at the chair.

Lorde's kitten-soft ears perked up, and her tail lifted and stiffened. Her nose twitched double time. She marched over to the ghost and stared. Hard.

Not quite a point, but we'd had Lorde since she was a puppy. Lu knew what Lorde was doing.

"This is nice," Lu said. Regret she couldn't hide weighed down her words. "But I'd like to see the other room."

"Oh," Dot nodded. "I suppose, if you'd like. It's a little smaller, doesn't have quite as much view."

"This is a little more than I need," she said wistfully.

She liked this room. Dammit.

"It's okay, Lorde. Tell her it's a Friendly."

I hadn't even tried contact with the ghost yet, so I was lying out my face.

Ghosts couldn't always see me. It had struck me as odd at first, but hey, I was not fully in any state of existence. I'd come to accept, and sometimes use to my advantage, the fact I could sneak up on people. Living and dead.

Lorde's tail wagged and she panted. Her face broke into a happy smile, black tongue only sticking out a little bit.

Lu paused, halfway out the door. Her eyebrows went up. "Um… On second thought, I changed my mind."

"Oh?" Dot paused, a new brass key already pulled out of her pocket and at the ready.

"Yes. I think maybe this will be good," Lu said. "It's very calming."

Dot beamed. "Thank you. I restored it myself. With help from my son and daughter, but all the furnishings and colors were my idea. I just wanted it to feel…peaceful. Like a garden in the shade."

Lu was quiet, watching Lorde lean in and sniff the chair. Well, sniff the ghost who still hadn't opened her eyes.

"It was my sister's room when we were growing up." Dot seemed perfectly comfortable filling the silence. She bustled over to the window, raised the wooden blinds, then opened the narrow closet door.

"She passed years ago. But I think she'd approve of the new look. Extra linens in here. This is your key." She handed over the brass key. "If you need anything, just ring the bell out in the main room. I'll hear it and be with you in a jiffy. If that doesn't work, text the main number. I'll get that too."

Lu nodded. "Thank you."

Dot made a quick exit while Lu looked across the room, out the window at the view of trees and grass and a little brick house across the street. She shut the door and put the key in her pocket. She waited, tracking the sound of Dot's footsteps, heart, breathing. When she was satisfied Dot was out of earshot, she turned to face the chair. "Who is it?"

The question was for me, but Lorde wagged her tail and moved back to sit next to Lu, tipping her furry face up and gazing adoringly at her.

"Let's find out," I said.

I strolled through the queen-size bed—new mattress, Egyptian cotton and all—stopping in front of the chair. I inhaled, exhaled in a thin stream, and drew my shoulders down like I was ready to lift the back of a truck.

I pulled energy and focus and *will*, dragging them to me like a heavy rope through the mud and rain, a sort of mental hand over hand that made sweat pop out on my upper lip. Then I shoved that focus, that *intent* into my words, throwing it like a javelin, screaming through a bullhorn to breach my world and impact the ghost's world.

It wasn't as hard as trying to influence the living world, but it still took a hell of a lot of effort.

"Afternoon," I said, that word hitting like a hammer on a single pane of glass.

The woman, who had the same round face and short nose as Dot, opened her eyes.

"What's your name?" I asked.

She screamed. At volume. When she ran out of breath, she clutched the knitting to her chest and gulped air, her eyes all buggy.

"Easy," I said in the crack of silence, "hang on. I'm not going to—"

But she'd already refueled. The shriek that came out of her could peel skin off an elephant.

"Jesus, lady." I stumbled back, one hand patting air, as if there were an "off" switch I could punch, the other cupped over my ear, trying to keep what was left of my brains in my noggin. "Calm down!"

Screamer rushed to her feet with unsettling speed. She fisted the knitting needles into stabbing position and pulled her arm back. The sock attached to the needles unrolled like a long, thin, unevenly striped tongue.

She paused for breath again.

"I don't want to hurt you!" I yelled. "I'm friendly. A friend. For the love of all the gods, stop screaming!"

For six whole, blissful, *silent* seconds, I thought I'd gotten through to her. I knew it was a hell of a shock to have someone that was not a ghost appear in the ghostly plane, but she was acting like I was there to kill her.

Which, technically, okay, I could be. But the energy it took to send a ghost packing meant glyphing magic and using enough of it to knock a spirit loose. I didn't have the time, energy, or inclination for any of that.

"All right," I said. "Good. So, I was just passing through and wondered if you…"

Her eyes narrowed, one hand fluttered up to her

throat, the other cocked at her shoulder, ready to lay the hammer down. Well, stab the knitting needles down.

Lorde decided it was time to get between us and bark her head off.

"Evil!" the ghost screamed. "Die!" She let out a battle cry and those knitting needles were finally on the move.

I rocked to the balls of my feet, ready to rush.

But the ghost was bullet fast. She swung, knitting needles aimed for the center of my chest, a chakra point. She had good instincts and aim. If those needles had any magic in them, I'd be in pain.

Instead, I jagged to one side, trying not to trip through Lorde who snapped at the ghost, getting nothing but a muzzle of air.

Lu strode over. "What is it? Who is it?" she demanded. Anger rolled off her in a familiar wave that made me lean toward her, wanting even that emotional connection, if it was all I could have.

The ghost took another swing. The needles *whooshed* right through me—

—and so did the rest of the ghost.

For a moment, we *adhered*, stuck in each other's skin, fully on each other's plane.

Every instinct told me to move, to run, to jerk away from that intimate touch, that vulnerable sharing of knowledge. But if I did anything too quickly, I could tear the ghost to shreds, and leave me in all kinds of lasting pain.

I held very still, claiming this space where our worlds merged, where we merged, grounding myself to the ghost's realm of existence while staying grounded in my own.

She must have felt it, the hard focus of my thoughts and *intent* to support her, keep her vital, to protect her from the stupid thing she'd just done.

She stopped, reaching for my intent, and that was enough for the connection to complete.

I knew I had seconds to tell her how she and I were going to get out of this bear trap she'd gotten us into without either of us springing the teeth.

I also wanted to avoid the download of each other's lives and memories.

That had only happened to me once, early on in this not-quite-dead life of mine. I'd rather it never happened again.

"My name's Brogan Gauge," I said. "I didn't mean to frighten you. I apologize if I did. My wife is staying in this bedroom, and I wanted to know the locals she might be spending the night with."

She hadn't said anything, but she wasn't screaming or trying to pull away. So far so good.

"Since you're a ghost, and I'm not quite dead, occupying the same space as we are can be a little tricky. If we try to part too quickly, it's gonna hurt a hell of a lot and neither of us are going to be the better for it."

I could feel the moment she understood what I was saying. She knew it was the truth because the windows between our minds and souls were slowly cracking open, and my thoughts were leaking out, easy for her to hear.

I heard hers, too, though I didn't want to. I had enough pain and guilt and anger in my long, long lifeish. I didn't need to be carrying someone else's along with mine.

"What's your name?" I asked.

Her thoughts tumbled, faint voices: a woman's, a man's, calling her name in a hundred different tones. Most of them happy, most of them good. But a few...a few were rage.

Family was a complicated thing.

"Stella," she said. I was surprised at her soft and lovely voice.

"Stella," I repeated as her memories washed by me. If I kept my vision sort of soft focused, I wouldn't have to see her—

—playing in the creek, tadpoles tickling her ankles—

—jumping on the back of a boy with broad shoulders and laughing as he spun her around and around until she was dizzy and clinging—

—the road, the rain, all the blood—

—her sister crying at the funeral home—

—memories.

I inhaled, exhaled, letting the emotional wave that came with each of those memories wash over me. It wasn't easy. Emotions had a way of lingering and leaving a stain. I'd wondered if part of why so many ghosts roamed the world was because of those emotions, anchoring them to the world, locking them down, feeling by feeling.

"So we're going to be just fine, Stella. We're both going to be just fine. All we have to do is agree to let go of each other. Best way to think of this is we're gonna move back one step, holding our arms out, fingers stretched."

Truth was, I didn't know the best way to do this. I'd only gotten stuck with one other ghost and had made it a point to avoid repeating that experience ever since.

I glanced down at Lorde, who had dropped into a sit and was watching me closely, her head tipping side-to-side with curiosity.

"Is he okay?" Lu asked, her anger still roiling around her, hot like a fire I wanted to draw up against, wanted to feel on my skin, my fingers, my lips. "Brogan, are you okay?" Her fingers drifted upward, hovering over the pocket watch hanging from that too-heavy chain on her too-delicate neck.

"No, don't, Lu. Not now. It's okay. Don't waste the minutes."

But she had that look on her face, jaw set with determination, eyes narrowed.

"Tell her no, Lorde. Lorde, tell her I'm okay. Tell her not to touch the watch."

Lorde tipped her head, then she yipped and wagged her tail.

Lu paused. "Yes or no Brogan, and you'd better be pretty damn clear, because I'm about to tap in and kick some ass."

Gods. Being dead made for messy communication.

"I need a favor," I told Stella. "I need to tell my wife not to try to enter this realm."

Stella was startled and curious about that statement, but remained silent.

"Three…" Lu warned.

"All I need you to do is trust me. I'm going to reach

out and tell her we're okay. It might sting, but I promise you, it won't harm you or me. It's temporary, okay?"

She nodded, which was weird since our heads were connected and I hadn't moved mine.

"Two…"

"Thank you," I said. "All right, so just hold real still, Stella. I'm going to stretch my thoughts and focus. Like I said, it will sting a little."

"One…"

I pulled my thoughts, my will, my mind together, and imagined an arrow, a dart, a needle, bright and sharp, piercing through the air, puncturing it with a muted "*tock*," opening that tiny space. And into that space, my thoughts, my will, my words burned bright, loud, full of my need, and the lonely want for her I could never hide.

"I'm okay."

Distantly, I heard Stella hiss, the sting of me reaching out across yet another plane burning through us.

Lu's breath hitched, her eyes opening, her mouth soft. "Brogan?"

Lorde yipped again, happy.

But Lu's gaze was on me. Right on me. My voice had given her the exact position where I was standing, and she knew. Knew I was there.

"Hey, baby," I said, even though she couldn't hear me now. "I love you."

She smiled, knowing I could see her. Knowing I was right there. "Hey." She reached out, and I couldn't help myself. I took her hand in mine.

Well, in mine and Stella's.

"I got this," I told her. "We're good."

Lorde got up and sniffed a circle around our feet, then sat, tail wagging.

"If that ghost is giving you a problem, let me know. I have salt and iron in the duffle, not to mention a few other items."

Stella jerked at that, but I soothed her. "She's joking. Well, she's not joking. She really has those things in her duffle. But she wouldn't use them unless I told her to. How's the sting?"

Stella refocused on our condition. "Better," she said.

"Good. So now that Lu isn't going to try to get in the middle of this, let's get us untangled. Ready?"

"No."

Ah, shit.

"Stella, this isn't something that I can hold for long. The plane that ghosts exist upon and the one that I travel aren't aligned exactly. Even if we didn't want it to, they're going to pull apart. And when they do that, they pull us apart too."

"How long before that happens?"

"I don't know. I've only been in this situation once, and I didn't wait that long before bailing ship."

"I want a favor," she said.

"Fair."

"I want to talk to my sister."

It took me a second to figure out who she was talking about, but then an image, a memory of a much younger Dot, the owner of the house, filled my vision.

"So, Dot's your sister?"

"Yes."

"This was the house you grew up in together?"

"This was my room." She didn't sound upset that Dot had remodeled it and was renting it out, but ghosts could be tricky. The ghosts I'd run across had lost big swaths of the things that went into being human. Most of them had dissolved down into just a handful of their strongest emotions, memories, or wants.

There were exceptions to that rule, but Stella felt like she was on her way to losing some of those things. Losing bits of her personality that she'd naturally built and changed and grown when she was alive.

"Maybe I can give your sister a message?" I had no idea how I was going to do that, but I'd try. "It isn't going to be easy. If the living aren't ready to hear from a ghost, it can be pretty hard on them. Are you sure this message is worth it?"

"She needs to know. I have to tell her. Let me tell her. She needs to know." Her emotions were boiling up, hot, heavy lava, smothering out my breathing room.

"All right. She needs to know. I'll find a way to get her a message."

"No. Not you. Me. Only me. *I* need to tell her."

"That's....more than I can promise, Stella."

Her anger was a hard slap that would have left my nose bleeding if I were flesh and blood.

"I know things," she said. "I...I saw your memories. You're looking for answers."

She had my full attention. "Be very clear with me."

"I saw your...thoughts? She's your wife, Lu? And

you want to be with her, but she's a…some kind of monster?"

"Lu's no kind of monster."

"But she's not human. Not anymore. Not since that horrible attack—"

"I was there," I said. "What does this have to do with talking to your sister?"

"It was thirty years ago, I think. Time's hard for me. But a man came through town. Riding the road. He had things to sell."

I didn't see how a carpetbagger fit into this conversation.

"Magic things," she said.

"Lots of people say they have magic things. Most of them are lying."

"I know, but this…I know it was magic, Brogan. I saw what it could do."

We didn't have much time. The movement between our planes was starting to change, like the second hand of two clocks ticking away at slightly different rhythms.

"What was it?" I asked.

"A journal. Small. Made out of leather and wood and metal and bone. He showed it to me. The man. Then he opened it to a page and called rain right out of the sky."

Trick. Lots of easy ways to make that happen without magic.

She must have been following my thoughts.

"It was a clear sky, Brogan. I might be dead, but I'm not that gullible." She dragged the memory out and shook it like snapping a rug.

And there I was, standing in the parking lot of the Dixie Truck Stop, clear blue sky buttoning down the edge of every horizon I could see.

The man was short, maybe only four and a half feet at best, and dressed in a tailored, pinstriped suit.

He didn't look like a god to me, nor could I tell from her memories if he were some other creature. Stella had assumed he was human, so that's how she remembered him.

Assumption went a long way toward monsters—human and otherwise—hiding in plain sight.

He drew the little book out of his breast pocket. It was the length of his hand and narrow, but even in a ghostly memory that thing shone.

It was magic. Stella was convinced of it.

I tried to look past her assumption. The book was a soft, tawny brown, worked with gold threads and bits of stone and metal. The hook was a bone carved into the shape of a bird in full dive, the loop of leather clutched in its talons.

He did something with the clasp, and the bird's talons flexed and released the leather.

A nice bit of hinge work there.

I couldn't see the writing on the page, but had the impression the paper was red, which seemed strange. Then the man recited something that sounded like a poem.

It was not a poem. Or at least it was not a human poem. It was a Faefolk song. Beautiful, haunting, and undeniably magical.

The sky boiled with clouds, white into gray, into chalkboard black.

The rain fell.

Hard, marble-sized droplets poured over the parking lot, the strange man, and the much younger Stella.

"How much?" the memory of Stella asked. "I can pay. I can pay you anything."

The man lifted one thick eyebrow, his eyes gone steely and cruel. "Anything?"

"Oh, Stella," I said, knowing what she must have promised. Her life. Maybe her soul. "Is that why you're here, stuck between the living world and those places beyond?"

"What are you saying?" she sounded annoyed. "What do you think I traded?" And before I could censor any of my thoughts, which was getting harder and harder by the minute, the second, she barked out a laugh.

A real, happy laugh.

"He wanted half a million dollars," she said, mirth giving her voice a burry warmth. "I wouldn't have offered my soul to anyone. I've read the Bible. I know Satan wears plain clothes."

"Well, if that was Satan, he upgraded to a pinstriped suit."

"Instead of paying, I stole it."

I blinked. Blinked again. "You what?"

"Stole the magic book."

"But…what about what the Bible says?"

"You think Satan should have a magic book,

Brogan? Because I don't think Satan should have a magic book."

"He wasn't…All right. No, I don't think Satan should have a magic book, but I don't think that was Satan."

She/we shrugged. "What matters is I have a book. A magic book. You can have it if you let me talk to my sister."

I/we lifted a hand and rubbed at my forehead. A headache was starting there, a real banger. I was out of time. Which meant I needed to choose.

Best choice: tell Stella no, and move on down the road.

"I'll scream," she said casually. "The entire time your wife and you are in this room. I'll scream. The entire time you are in this town, I'll follow you around screaming."

Oh, good gods.

Worst choice: find a way for her to talk to her sister and get that magic book.

Lu could send it up to Mr. Headwaters, the antique dealer who was always on the lookout for magical items.

Or maybe it had something in it that would help us. Maybe the Faefolk had a spell or a curse or a song that would break our soul problem.

Maybe it would heal us.

Maybe it would point us toward the monsters who had done this to us.

Maybe it would put enough money in the bank account, Lu wouldn't have to worry about that broken down silver truck and could buy herself a more reliable vehicle.

Maybe it would just give us an ending.

All viable routes.

I puffed out a breath. "All right," I said. "Fine. You have a deal. I'll find a way to get a message to your sister—"

"No, I want to talk to her. You find a way for *me* to talk to her."

"Right. You get to talk to her and in return, you give the book to Lu and me. Deal?"

"Deal."

She was buzzing with a tsunami of emotions I didn't want to surf.

"Time to step apart," I said. "Remember how?"

"Take one step back, my arms out straight, fingers stretched."

"That's it. It will feel a little like trying to pull a tight boot off by the heel."

Her main emotion turned into determination.

"Ready?"

"Yes, I am."

I set my feet, adding my will to my own *here* and *now* and *real* while Stella took a big breath and held it like she was ready to dive off the cliff into a river way, way down there.

She stepped back—

—*fire burned through me, hot enough I froze, every inch of me screaming in agony*—

I leaned forward, gently, slowly.

It wasn't so much like a boot being pulled off as it was like being skinned alive.

It was too much. Pain filled all of me. Consciousness was a speck out there, glinting in the distance. I was losing hold, shaking apart.

Then it was done.

I fell to my knees, panting, sweat dripping off me like that Fae-born rainstorm. The world swayed and my stomach squirmed.

I barfed, and even though I didn't eat, the energy that fueled me came up in a putrid, steaming puddle.

I hung my head and breathed through my mouth, not wanting to smell my own sick.

"That wasn't so bad." Stella's voice was more distant, as if she'd stepped into another room, closed all the doors and windows, and was shouting just to be heard through the thick layers. "Just like pulling off a boot—easy."

I groaned, because I was pretty sure the boot didn't think so.

CHAPTER SEVEN

"Three days, tops." Sunshine wiped his hands on a clean cloth, leaving greasy streaks behind.

Lu nodded, her eyes focused on the truck parked in the closest slot in the bay, the hood up and blocks behind its wheels.

"How much?"

"We'll have to figure in time, but just the part for a blown radiator is gonna come in around two hundred. Timing chain's that at least. Then labor and there's a few other things I'd recommend we do while we've got it."

"He's gonna try to rip you off." I was leaning on a tool box, facing both of them. That way I could stare over Lu's shoulder through the window that showed the hall, and just enough of the doorway to the office I could see Jo, working on her laptop.

She glanced up, took a nice long stare at Sunshine's

back and shoulders, then shook her head as if trying to talk herself out of something.

I was curious.

"I'm thinking new transmission fluid would be good, and oil and air filter." He held up a donut-shaped part, angling it so she could see the dirt and crud clogging it. "A front end alignment if you have the budget for it. Other than that, I don't see any immediate trouble."

"Nothing?" Lu asked.

I pushed off the tool box and moved straight on through the walls separating the work space and the office.

"You'll need to be thinking about tires soon," I heard Sunshine say. "And you need a spare. I've got a couple out back we can set you up with. Nothing fancy, but I'll throw it in for free. Struts aren't great, but they'll do you for a few months."

"And how much will that put me back?"

I didn't hear the answer because I was through the hall and in the office.

Jo had the music playing low, some sweet-voiced woman singing about going down to the river. The window air conditioner was doing the work to knock the early afternoon heat right in the teeth, and the bottle of soda on the desk sweated on top of a short stack of napkins.

Jo muttered to herself, chewing on her lip, then letting go and clacking the stud in her tongue against the back of her teeth.

"What is wrong with you?" she muttered. "I've run the diagnostics. Wireless is here. It just keeps cutting out.

Why? There's nothing out here to block the signal. Is it the building?" She glanced up at the walls and back to the router that sat on the desk, a pile of paper on each side. "Crappy wiring? Someone hacking in to get their share without the boss man knowing?"

She leaned back a bit and her gaze clicked right out the office door to the bay where Sunshine stood, one hand in his back pocket, thumb and pinky spread over that cheek, his other hand gesturing with the rag toward the truck.

"Not that Fisher would allow crappy workmanship around here," she scoffed. "I mean, look at him."

I stepped up right next to her, turned, and looked at him.

"I don't get it," I said.

She hummed.

I tried again. "What do you think about him?"

I was pretty sure what she was going to say. That he was a hick, a redneck, a country boy with more grease and beer in his veins than blood. That he was ornery and chauvinistic, and not worth a second look.

But a second look she gave him.

"You like him?" I pushed a little harder, incredulous.

"No," she said. "No more jumping into things. That's how I ended up back in maintenance. And I refuse to give that asshole Brett the satisfaction of seeing me fail."

So that was…not very informative. She'd been demoted? By Brett? Or was Brett a boyfriend, brother, friend?

"You like him," I stated.

She picked up her soda and ran her thumb through the condensation. "I am not going to get involved because I am not that dumb. He was an ass. He told me I work for a crap company, which—okay, Brett is a dick. And Calvin's..." she shrugged. "Whatever that is with Red Sonya out there."

"He's not flirting with her," I said. Calvin leaned close to Lu and told her something like it was a secret. Lu laughed. No, Lu giggled. I hadn't heard that sound out of her in months.

Jo scoffed and chugged down the soda. "Fuck him anyway."

"Atta girl," I said. "Fuck him. Well, don't actually. You're worth more than a pretty face and a pair of greasy hands."

"Right in here," Sunshine said, as he followed Lu toward the office.

Jo's face had done a remarkable blank-slate make over. She was clacking away at the keys of her computer like she hadn't looked up in an hour.

Sunshine opened the door like a gentleman and stepped aside so first Lorde, then Lu could enter. Lorde tipped her head up at me and wagged her tail, then settled down on the opposite side of the desk.

Lu looked happy, her face flushed and those hard lines across her forehead and at the corners of her eyes smoothed away.

She was up to something.

"Cupid is still a god, Lu," I said. "Still dangerous. So is Fate. Do you really want to get us mixed up in god business?"

"Hey, Jo," Lu said, all friendly. "How's the repair going?"

Sunshine lingered by the door, holding the rag in both his hands and looking nervous. He glanced at Jo, looked down at his boots, then pulled his shoulders back, forward, then back again. He threw glances at the computer and out the little window with the air conditioner stuck in the bottom of it.

"It's fine," Jo said. If a CLOSED sign could talk, it'd sound just like that.

"Is there anything you need?" Lu pressed. "That diner down the street Calvin recommended was really good."

"I'm on the clock," she said, still not looking up. I was pretty sure she was peeking sideways at Sunshine.

Lu shot a look Calvin's way and lifted one eyebrow.

He took a big breath, then let go of the rag so it was hanging from one hand. "I was thinking," he said. "That maybe you and I, maybe we could…"

"Hold up there, champ," I said. "She's working. On your crappy technology. You stuck your boot in your mouth this morning. She deserves an apology. Or better, she deserves you to just walk away."

"…the diner's real nice," Calvin was still saying. "Uh…I know the owners…"

"Sorry, Lu," I said. "This thing isn't going to work."

"…and everyone's gotta eat." He winced. "I mean, I'm headed out to lunch and thought you could use a break too. Thought maybe we could…"

"Not a chance, Sunshine. She's busy." I dropped one hand on the computer, the other on the router. Sometimes I could get the feel of a thing, of what was broken in it.

"…would you?" Calvin yammered. "I'd like to buy you lunch. For all the hard work you're doing here. And to apologize for the rough start this morning."

I shoved my fingers into the router, feeling around for heat and cold and the strange discordant waves of electricity traveling as packets of data. Took me all of a half second to find a blank spot where electricity wasn't flowing. I figured that was where things had gone gunny bag.

"Gotcha." I focused, willing that blank spot to carry the electricity, which wasn't easy. In for a pound plus a penny.

"I don't think…" Jo said.

"If you don't want to go out for it, that's okay too," Sunshine said. "You can order in. On me. Because I… uh…really appreciate you doing…this." He sort of waved the rag at the desk.

I pulled hard, forcing the electricity to surge.

The was a *pop*, there was a *snap, snap, snap*, and then there was smoke rising up out of the router case.

"Holy shit!" Jo pushed back.

I groaned. Lu just looked at the router, looked at Lorde, who sat up and stared at me. Lu rotated so she was facing me. A little smug smile curved her lips as she crossed her arms over her chest.

I should have been angry, frustrated, but that smile was honey on the flower's petal. It was sunlight pouring soft through the clouds.

Even if it was an I-know-what-you-tried-to-do smirk.
God, I loved her.

"Fine," I said. "It didn't work. That doesn't mean
Sunshine over there is dating Jo. You haven't won."

Lu gave me one slow blink and her smile widened.
Not enough to show teeth, but I knew she was laughing
at me.

"I got this," Sunshine said. "Hang on." He strode
toward the exact space where I was standing, so I
walked through the desk and stood next to Lorde.

"You're on my side, aren't you girl?" I asked her.

She wagged her tail faster, her black tongue hanging
out as she looked from me to Lu and back to me.

"I'll get rid of this." Sunshine picked up the router,
deftly unplugged it, and strode quickly out of the room,
taking the stink of burned wires with him.

"So," Lu said, "you think it might be an electrical
problem?"

Jo lifted both eyebrows, half a smile turning her
golden brown face sharp, her eyes sparkling. She looked
like a woman who liked mischief: starting it, getting into
it, and keeping it going.

"Electrical's a possibility."

Lu stuck her hands in her front pockets. "If you
want me to tell Calvin you'd rather go to lunch with me,
or alone, or not at all, I will. I think he wants to make up
for that 'crap company' and Texas thing. But you don't
owe him anything. Not even lunch."

Jo stood and picked her messenger bag up off the
floor, pulling it on so the strap ran across her chest and

the bag rested against one hip. "He was an ass this morning."

"He was."

"But he seems…decent."

"He does."

"You get along with him."

"I do."

"And hey, free food, right?" She gathered a few pieces of equipment off the desktop.

"Free food's good," Lu said. "But not if it comes with strings attached."

"Oh, I can handle myself."

"I see that." Lu snapped her fingers once for Lorde to come up beside her. "I'm just saying you don't have to."

"You wanna join us?" she asked.

"Say no," I said. "Come on, Lu. You got them a lunch date. That's enough. Isn't that enough?"

"Sure," Lu said. "I could eat." She smiled, showing white teeth, the canines just slightly sharper than normal.

Sunshine strode back into the office. "That's in the trash where it won't burn anything down. Go ahead and step out for awhile so the office can air out." He walked the long way around the desk so he didn't have to squeeze past her, then turned off the air conditioner and did something with the upper part of the window to open it a crack.

"If you decide on lunch, put it on my tab," he said. "Susan knows me. She'll set you right up."

He was moving around the office, unplugging cords

from the wall, turning off the surge protector, and fiddling with the light switch to make the ceiling fan rotate the right way.

"Good?" he asked, over his shoulder.

Jo shrugged. "Lu could use a bite to eat too. How about we all go together?"

Sunshine stopped. I could feel the hope that radiated off him. Like he'd been walking down the dust and heat of the road for days and finally spotted a river running clear and clean.

"I'd like that," he said with so much heart in his voice no one could have missed it.

I tipped my eyes to the sky. "It's not my fault," I said to Cupid. "No one could have talked Lu out of this. Not even you."

Cupid didn't reply. I hadn't expected him to. The gods largely ignored us—just one more human tragedy in a world full of them—so Lu and I largely ignored them.

It was better that way.

"I'll let Ray know we'll be out," Sunshine said.

"Good," Jo replied.

"Great," he said, looking at her like she'd just handed him a puppy and his favorite cone of ice cream.

Jo stood there studying him. Those dimples, those sky-filled eyes, that smile that poured out summer and sunlight, easy music and slow moving warm waters.

"Lunch?" Lu's happy tone broke the spell.

Jo came back to herself with a little start. Sunshine grinned harder at the slight rise of color in her cheeks.

"I'll be right there," he said.

Jo strolled out of the office, Lu and Lorde drifting behind her.

"Great," I said.

CHAPTER EIGHT

I 'd seen a lot of people fall in love. Sometimes the fall was slow and easy, growing out of years of friendship, of familiarity. Sometimes it was a lightning bolt strike: fast, furious, and scorching hot.

But most of the time, falling in love was a mix of things. A collection of moments. That one joke, those two songs, that third meal, that fourth walk when gazes locked and didn't look away.

When a soul reaches out and another soul answers back.

Lu had seen just as many falling hearts. She had an eye for it, truth be told. Could see when two people were hoping, wanting. Could sense loneliness like an old, dusty song scratching out into the empty and waiting for the echoed harmony.

And when Lu got her teeth into something she thought she could fix, she wasn't an echo, she was a damned bullhorn.

"You live in Texas?" Lu dragged a fried pickle through the little paper cup of sauce: dip, drag, dip, drag.

Jo finished chewing a bite of burger. "Not really."

Lu raised her eyebrows.

"I'm here now. I'm traveling. Looking for a place." She very carefully didn't look over at Sunshine, who was forking down a salad with lots of taco fixings and a river of hot sauce running through it.

"That smoking router mean you're staying a night?" He was all casual and cool now, the diner a familiar enough place, lunch a neutral enough ground, he'd gotten his feet back under him.

Lorde was outside lounging in the shade of the tree. When Susan—owner and hostess of MaryJo's—had seen the dog, she'd produced two bowls, one for water, one for "ends and bits" that turned out to be chicken meat, some fresh boiled eggs, and kibble with a nice, juicy beef bone sticking up out of it.

Lorde couldn't be happier. Well, she'd probably prefer to be in the diner with us, but she was just a few steps away from the building. I could get to her in an instant if Lu needed her.

"Not sure," Jo said. "By the time I drive down to Springfield to get whatever router we have in stock, it's going to be late. You close at six, right?"

"I can stay if you want to come back tonight," he offered.

"Do it," I said to her. "Put in the new router and be on your way. This small town isn't where your life is headed. You want bigger things, remember?"

I could tell my words had some influence on her. Enough she frowned and took a drink of her cola.

Lu must have felt my words too.

"You could drive down in the morning," Lu said. "The place I'm renting has a spare room. Quiet. Good price."

Sunshine leaned back and picked up the huge glass of lemonade, draining it by half in one go. "Since it's on me that you'd have to make the drive and stay an extra night, you can put the hotel cost on my bill."

"Don't fall for those dimples," I said. "Get outta Dodge and come back tomorrow."

"I could just come back tomorrow," she said.

"Great idea!" I clapped my hands. "Now that it's settled…"

"Fisher, don't you move!" A man pushed past Susan and stopped at our table. He was short and built like a steamroller. His wide chest and broad belly might have once been muscle but were now going to fat. His suit jacket, dark trousers, and dress shoes were a step above affordable.

Thinning yellow hair, combed and sprayed, didn't do the job of covering up the bald spot on top.

Insurance? Cars? Time shares? He was some kind of salesman.

"You said you'd have that part in today." His voice was louder than necessary, making sure everyone in the place noticed when he spoke.

Sunshine leaned back a bit more, his body language opening up. He was squaring for a fight and happy to go the extra round.

"Doug. I'm on my lunch break. How about you stop by the shop in a half hour or so?"

"I'm stopping by now. When can I pick up my car?"

"I'll tell you that when I'm back at the shop. Which will be about a half hour or so."

Doug narrowed his eyes, then seemed to notice the other people at the table, especially Jo.

"Well, you sure aren't from around here, are you?" Doug gave Jo an insulting once over. "Do you speak English?"

"You're a horse's ass," I said.

Lu hadn't moved, but I could feel her tense, ready to spring.

Sunshine shifted his boots under the table, shoulders dipping, both hands going flat on either side of his plate. From the look on his face, he was going to pop Doug right in the nose.

Jo took her time chewing a fry, letting the uncomfortable silence spread out and out. "Not to an ass like you." She didn't even throw him a look.

Sales-schmuck's mouth opened, closed, and he turned a deep, dark red. He sputtered, head jerking back and forth, looking for allies among the diners.

People were watching, hell, it was probably the most interesting thing that had happened all month, being how small the town was. But no one was taking it on themselves to come to his defense.

Most of them were scowling at him.

Jo finished off her soda, then stood. "Thanks for lunch," she said to Lu and Sunshine.

Sunshine was watching her. It was a mix of respect

and humor, and yeah, if I was looking close enough, it might be desire too.

Lu noticed all that, probably better than I. "Do you want to check out that room?" she asked.

Jo shook her head. "Naw, I gotta hit the road if I'm going to get back before dark. Excuse me. Step aside, please."

Sales-schmuck dug in his heels. Leaned forward to tower over her, even though she had several inches on him. He wanted a fight. Wanted to take her down, put her under his shoe. Wanted to establish his dominance as something better.

As if any human being who behaved like a shit was better than a smart, strong woman like Jo.

Jo shifted the message bag, her hand dropping into a pocket. I figured she either had a sock full of nickels in there or a can of mace.

"Kick him in the pea shooter," I suggested.

"Move aside," Jo repeated, not backing down an inch.

The schmuck threw a glare at Sunshine.

"I'd move," Sunshine suggested. "'Cause you're making an ass out of yourself."

"Watch your mouth, Fisher." Doug jabbed a finger at him. But he finally stepped slightly to one side, not quite making enough room for Jo to get by.

She strode forward, shoulder-checking him hard enough Sales Schmuck had to take another step back.

Sunshine planted his elbow on the table and fanned his fingers around his mouth to hold back his chuckle.

"You better have my damn car ready by time I get

there," Doug snarled, his skin gone purple, sweat beading across his forehead.

"No, that's not going to happen now."

"What does that mean?"

"I don't need your business, Doug."

"Like hell you don't." Doug went on with his snarling while he stomped over to Susan and demanded a table.

I hoped Susan spit in his coffee.

"You're turning away his money?" Lu asked.

"I don't support people who can't treat other people like decent human beings."

"And you were going to pay for her to stay in town?" Lu asked, her eyes on Sunshine, watching every move.

"Sure. Better a fresh start in the morning than her having to put in overtime. I haven't had reliable internet for a couple weeks now. One more day wouldn't matter."

Lu listened to every word and all the things behind them. Even I could tell his casual tone covered more he didn't want to say. It covered confusion, mixed with surprise and a soft sort of loneliness.

"We don't do this, Lu," I said, sitting down in the seat Jo had left. "We don't meddle in love affairs. We hunt magical items. We sell magical items. We look for some way to break this half-alive curse we're living under. Love falls squarely under the rule of gods and mortals, not wayward souls like us."

Her fingers lifted toward the pocket watch resting against her heart. She didn't touch it, but I knew she wanted to. I knew she wanted to talk to me.

"Let's go, Lu. Let's hit the road. I don't think Jo wants anything to do with Sunshine, here. He just let her walk out that door."

"I'll settle the bill," Sunshine said, "and get to work on your truck. You can stop by anytime to check out the progress."

"I will."

He stood away from the table and paused to say something to Susan who was at the coffee station. She gave him a peck on the cheek, then he strolled out the door.

Lu stirred the ice in her glass with a straw, then drank the rest of her water. "He likes her," she whispered so that only I could hear.

I blew out a huge sigh. "I'm never gonna talk you out of this, am I? You playing Cupid."

Lu looked off into the distance, a small smile ghosting her lips.

"Wish I knew what was going through your head to put that look on your face." I leaned forward to crowd up into her space, wanting to be nearer to her, wanting to hold her, surround her, feel her. I drew one finger across the back of her hand, and she turned her hand over, letting my fingers slide between hers even though she couldn't feel it.

"They're talking," she whispered.

I frowned and looked around. "Who?"

That's when I spotted Sunshine standing outside the window with Jo.

"Oh, hell no." I stood and pushed through the wall, careful not to touch Lu on my way past.

There was a moment where the diner spoke to me—it was old, had seen fire, hard winds, floods. Flashes of those moments stuttered before my eyes, along with the echo of laughter, sobbing, and music that was popular during the jukebox fad.

Then I popped through to the outside.

Lorde lifted her head from where she still lay in the shade, gnawing on the soup bone.

"Stay, girl." I didn't want the dog to follow me and put an end to the conversation I planned to overhear.

Lorde looked between me and the restaurant, wagged her tail slowly, then went back to the bone.

"...think it's pretty clear, isn't it?" Jo said. She leaned against her car—a little GTO with great bones and a bad paint job. Sunshine was standing in front of her, hands stuck in his back pockets, smiling that smile.

"What, that Doug is a class-A jackass? Yeah, he's been that way since he moved back here ten years ago. We mostly ignore him."

"We?"

Sunshine shrugged. "The town McLean. We all know he's a crappy human."

She bit her bottom lip, trying to figure something there behind his words.

"You could stay," he said quieter, "for the night. Let me cover your room. Business expense. No personal strings attached."

"I don't think I fit in here."

"I'd rather have fifty of you over one of Doug."

Her eyebrows raised, and there was the slightest pinking of her cheeks.

"What I'm saying is, I'm sorry for him, and I hope you won't let the worst of us turn you away from the good we have here. If you'd like, stay the night. I mean, not with me. I'm not expecting you to…" His ears went red, and he leaned his shoulders back and stared at the trees on the other side of the parking lot.

"I'm not asking for…anything else." He blew out a breath and chuckled, wiping a hand over the back of his neck.

"Smooth moves, Champ," I said.

"It's like I've never spoken to a woman before," he muttered. "What I'm saying is, this is purely business despite the fact that I enjoy your company, Jo."

She had that focus in her gaze. She liked the look of him, liked his thoughtfulness, liked his awkwardness.

"You're looking for a new start," I reminded her as I leaned my ass against the car and rubbed a finger over a rusty spot. "What's a pit stop town like McLean got that makes you think you can build here?"

But from the softening of her body language, from the strong beat of her heart as she silently considered Sunshine and his offer, I knew exactly what this town had that was looking like a new start to her.

One handsome, sincere, slightly awkward mechanic, who could put his foot in his mouth, and be man enough to take it out again.

"Up to you," Sunshine said. "You can start off in the morning, be back here early afternoon. You'll have the rest of the day to fix it before you… go."

He swallowed, and I could see the desire in him, too, the need to be near her, the need for her to stay. But he didn't make another move, didn't crowd her up, just stood there, giving her time to think it over.

I grunted, grudgingly admitting he had boundaries.

Lu stepped out of the restaurant, and Lorde abandoned the bone to run over to her, wagging her tail for all she was worth.

I watched Lu stroll this way, facing the two of them like she knew what they were talking about (which she did) and happy they were working things out (which she was).

I couldn't keep my eyes off her. My wife, looking smug and maybe a little high-handed, but also happier than I'd seen her in a long, long time.

"Maybe it's time," I said to her. "Let the road go. Settle down in a place. Maybe it's time…" I almost said to stop looking. To give up on finding something that would fix us, change us, give us back a life once and for all.

But Lu's eyes narrowed. From the lift of her chin, I knew she was feeling the gist of what I was saying, and she was having none of it.

I sighed. "I know," I said. "We don't give up until we're both alive or the bastards are dead."

Lu's gaze skated the area and finally landed pretty close to where I sat, still leaning on the car.

I pushed off and stepped over to her, running my hands down her arms. "I hear you. I know. I know."

She blinked, then tipped her palm up. I took it, just as I always did. Just as I always would.

"So that room," Jo said, when Lu moved a little closer to them. "It still open?"

Lorde stopped next to Sunshine, who bent and gave her a good scratching behind her ears. When he raised his head toward Lu, there was nothing but hope blazing in his eyes.

Lu smiled at Jo. "Let's find out."

CHAPTER NINE

Lu and Jo strolled up the B&B steps, but before they reached the door, Lorde pushed past them to stand right in front of Lu, her nose almost touching the door, her ears flicked back.

That was all the warning I needed.

I dipped my shoulders so I didn't hit either woman and slid through the door sideways.

For just a moment, I caught old voices of women, a man's laugh, and the giggling of children long grown and gone, but I didn't pause to sort out the house's memories.

Something was wrong. Wrong enough, Lorde was in protection mode.

As soon as I stepped into the living room-turned-lobby, I knew what it was.

Or rather, who.

The hunter stood on one side of the visitor desk, Dot stood on the other, her back to the wall.

To say she was intimidated by his size and body language would be doing Dot a disservice. She didn't look afraid, but she did look cautious and annoyed.

"Just the night?" she asked, obviously stalling.

The hunter was a big man. Big enough people probably looked up when he entered a room.

But I was bigger. And I knew there were ways to carry a big body, ways to give off signals that big didn't mean angry, or violent, or dangerous.

He wasn't putting any effort into downplaying his size, looming as he was over the smaller woman.

"Don't rent to this asshole, Dot." I crossed the space so I stood next to her, shoulder to not-quite-touching shoulder.

The asshole's dark eyes flicked my way.

Interesting.

"Yeah?" I said. "You can hear me? Well, then listen real close. You are not welcome here. Fuck off."

His gaze wandered across the wall behind me, like a blind spider tracking a fly by feel alone.

"Maybe two," he replied to Dot, finally looking her way again.

"Not happening," I said. "Don't do it, Dot."

I widened my stance and shook out my hands. Lu came striding into the room like she owned the place and rent was overdue.

"Hello," Dot said, relieved to see her. "Welcome back."

Lu didn't even pause in her stride, she stepped past the hunter who had the sense to turn her way as soon as the door had opened.

"I don't like how you're looking at her, ass," I said. "You touch her, she's gonna break your neck, and I'm gonna finish off whatever soul you have left."

Lu ignored the hunter like he was invisible. "Jo was just wondering if she could pick up the key to her room now."

Yeah, Lu had good hearing. She knew Dot didn't want to rent the extra room to the hunter.

"Right, Jo?" Lu gestured her forward.

Jo sauntered over like she'd been here for weeks. "Sorry I wasn't by earlier. Thanks for letting me reserve the room over the phone."

Dot glanced from Lu to Jo to the hunter, and then back to Lu. Jo had not reserved the room on the phone.

"Come on, Dot. Be smart," I said. "Go for the nice punk rock girl and ditch this joker."

"Not a problem at all," Dot said. She dug the key out of the drawer and held it out for Jo. "Sorry to say that's my last room." She smiled sweetly at the hunter.

He nodded, the corner of his lip twisting as he chewed the inside of his cheek. "Looks like you got the drop on me." He nodded at Jo, but his eyes ticked over to Lu and turned cold.

Lu just held his gaze.

"Thanks again," Jo palmed the key and moved out of the blast zone of the glaring contest. "Lu, I can show you that program you wanted to see now."

There was no program, but I had to hand it to her. She had good instincts and knew when to back up a friend to get her away from a dangerous situation.

"Take a hike, hunter," I said. "These women are

more than capable of knocking your teeth out. Don't make them humiliate you."

His hands twitched, as if he'd heard that. Or heard part of it, anyway.

Fine by me. He wouldn't be the first human sensitive to ghosts, the undead, or whatever sort of thing I was.

"Sure," Lu said. "I got nothing better to do." She gave the hunter one up-down look, then turned her back on him and walked down the hall, discreetly guiding Jo toward the room while letting the hunter know he wasn't worth her time.

"I think you can find a room at the Super 8," Dot suggested.

He seemed to remember she was in the room and sniffed. "Yeah."

Then he turned and was out the door.

I followed him all the way to his truck. Got in the passenger side while he sat in the driver's. He didn't start the engine for several minutes, just sat there watching the house.

"And people think ghosts are creepy," I muttered.

Finally, he pulled out his phone and thumbed through his contacts. He pressed dial and held the phone against his ear.

"It's here," he said.

I leaned in to hear the other side of the conversation. Just like the wireless router, electronics and me didn't always mix, so I was careful not to touch the phone. All I could make out was it was a woman's voice.

"Yes," Hunter said. Then he disconnected the call.

"That was not helpful," I said. "You working for

someone? Who? You hunting for someone? One of the werewolf clans? One of the government agencies? You hunting for monsters? Gods? Or are you just hunting for magic? Who's your boss?"

He sat there through every word, just staring at the house, eyes shifting from window to window.

"You touch any of those women, and I will tear through reality and turn you inside out. Understand?"

I pushed that last word, filled it with my anger and sheer, pig-headed determination.

If he heard it, he showed no sign.

He just started the truck, backed up and drove to the Super 8.

I stuck with him while he checked in, walked to the room, and tossed his duffel on the bed. I shoved my hand into the duffel and found clothes, toiletries, a gun cleaning kit, and explosives.

Interesting.

I waited for another hour, but all he did was take a shower—leaving a gun handy on the sink—then pulled the chair over to the window so he could stare out it.

When he closed his eyes and started breathing like he was asleep, I moved from the room and followed my soul back to my heart.

Lu was in her room. She sat in the middle of the bed, Lorde half draped across the quilt, her head in Lu's lap.

Lu wasn't looking out the window. Her eyes were closed. Other than her fingers slowly petting the softest spot behind Lorde's ears, she was perfectly still.

"Hey, love." I sat at the top of the bed, leaning

against the headboard. Lorde lifted her nose toward me and wagged her tail. Lu didn't open her eyes, but she smiled.

"You should get some sleep. I need to talk to you tonight."

Lu inhaled, exhaled, her shoulders relaxing by degrees.

I scrunched up, scooting forward so my chest was nearly touching her back. I reached around her and pressed one finger firmly on the pocket watch that hung against her heart. "Tonight." I made the word strong enough, I knew she felt it.

She pressed her fingers against the pocket watch, chasing the feel of me, even though my touch was already gone.

"Get some rest," I said again. "I'll keep an eye on you. And Jo."

Lorde wagged her tail again, thumping, thumping.

"There's a graveyard just on the west side of town," she said. "Good?"

"Tell her good, Lorde."

Lorde gave a short woof. Lu nodded. "All right. Let's get some sleep, girl."

I slid out of the way and watched Lu unlace her boots and shuck out of her jeans. She left her shirt on and climbed between the sheets, patting the side of the bed to tell Lorde to sleep there between Lu and the door. Lu settled on her side, facing the big window.

The blinds were closed, but sunlight still trickled through at the edges and corners.

"I got it," I repeated. "I'm right here." I eased down

into the chair—the one by the dresser, not the one in the corner that the ghost had been in.

Lou shifted and pressed her back against Lorde, who was already snoring softly.

I watched Lu drift off to sleep, dividing my attention between the slice of sky I could see out the window, and the rest of the room.

"I found it!" Stella appeared in the chair, her knitting once again in her lap. "I found the journal."

"Where is it?"

Stella looked exactly as I'd seen her earlier, except for the glint of determination in her eyes. "I want to talk to my sister first. Then I'll tell you where it is."

"That's not going to work, Stella. You could be lying."

"You could be lying too."

I shrugged. "Chance you take. Show me the journal, and I'll find some way for you to talk to your sister."

She frowned, working through the risk and reward. I'd had this conversation, or similar ones, with a variety of people and creatures over the years.

Me, I was dead. So there wasn't much on the line. It gave me leverage in negotiations most couldn't wield.

"How do I know I can trust you?" she asked.

"You don't. But if it's any solace, Lorde trusts you."

She studied the dog snoring happily on top of the bed in what had once been her own room.

"Lorde isn't worried about you," I went on, "so I'm not worried about you. Maybe you can't trust me, but dogs have a nose for quality people."

"You don't know how long I've waited for the chance to speak to her…"

"Don't talk to me about longing, Stella."

Something in my expression must have tipped her off that I had an intimate knowledge of the pain of waiting for someone you loved.

"You're right. I…I'll take you to it. To the journal. But I won't let you take it. You can't have it until I speak to her. Understand?"

"Yes."

"You give me your word?"

"Yes."

"Good. Good then." She stood and quick as a blink, flickered out and was standing in front of me.

Ghosts. Always showing off.

Lorde lifted her big bear of a head to assess the situation. Then she yawned and lowered her head with a snort.

Lu opened her eyes, staring toward the chair where I sat.

"It's okay, love," I said. "I'll be right back."

Lu closed her eyes again.

"Can she hear you?" Stella asked.

"No. But we've been together for a long time. She knows…well, she knows." I got to my feet and stretched, lifting my arms over my head and bending my elbow to pull at the catch between my shoulder blades.

Stella watched all that with interest. "You don't really feel sore do you?"

"Yep."

"But you are a…a…well, you're not alive. You don't have any muscles, blood, nerves left."

"I know I must have one nerve left because you're getting on it."

Stella covered her mouth and laughed. "You did not just say that."

I winked. "How about you show me that journal. If it's as magic as you think, it might have something that will help us figure out how you get to talk to your sister."

Her eyes widened. "Yes. Oh, yes, that's a wonderful idea! Can you turn pages? I don't have enough," she wiggled her hands, "solidness to do it. I've tried. If I had even half a hand, I'd have written Dot a note. Maybe dragged a word or two across a foggy mirror like the ghosts in those TV shows. Do you watch TV? Or *did* you when you were alive?"

Lorde had lifted her head again, listening to the barrage of words.

Ghosts were talky. It was like they haven't had anyone to talk to in a hundred years.

I tipped my chin at Lorde, and the dog got the hint and went back to lightly sleeping, her ears twitching at the subtle sounds of the old house settling in the sunlight, the brush and whisper of branches and leaves in the wind beyond the window.

"Or are you old enough to have only listened to radio? I can't tell by your clothes, but maybe you can change yours? I've been stuck in this same dress and shoes since the day of the…since the *day*. But I've never felt sore or stiff. I can't feel anything really."

She frowned again and held out her hands, giving

her fingers a wiggle. "I think it's a memory of sensation. I remember what it's like to touch something: fire's hot, ice is cold, but actually touching something isn't…it isn't the same. Of course nothing is the same."

"Where's the journal?" I asked. I was beginning to think I would have preferred she just follow me around screaming instead of this non-stop babbling. No wonder she had something to say to her sister. Stella was a talker.

"What? Oh. This way." She stepped through the exterior wall.

I followed, ignoring the house's memories of sunshine and wind and snow piled up so high, it covered the windows.

Stella waited for me right there next to the pecan tree. "You gave me your word."

"It hasn't changed. I see the journal, you get to talk to Dot."

She nodded, her sober eyes drinking down each word. "I'd forgotten… Well, I've forgotten a lot of things. You'd think with all the time I have, I'd be swimming in memories, but they seem to fade more and more. The journal wasn't where I remembered putting it the last time I touched it. But a lot has happened since then. I died."

She waited, so I nodded. "Do you remember that?" I asked.

"Every second."

"White light calling you up?"

She pressed her lips together and nodded. "There

were voices. Family, friends. My aunt Claire gave me a hug. She was…going to lead me, I think."

"And?"

I'd always been curious about the dead who stayed behind. All of them had at least one peaceful happy thing happen when they'd breathed their last. Seeing a family member, a friend, a beloved pet just waiting to take them into that warm light.

Not me. I'd emptied my lungs and come out of cold blackness to the sound of Lu screaming.

"I couldn't leave without Dot. Without telling her. Or…or being here when she dies."

"Solid," I said, letting her know I approved. "Where's the journal now?" I asked for what felt like the hundredth time.

"Oh. It's under the shed."

I looked around. Grass, trees, road, more grass. No shed.

"This way." She walked with a floaty stride around the side of the house to the back.

She didn't seem distressed or slowed by the distance from her room. Some spirits were stuck within certain geographical areas. It looked like her area covered at least the house and property around it.

"There. It's under there."

She pointed at what could generously be considered a shed but what I would have called a burn pile.

The whole structure had fallen in on itself, boards and bricks tumbled into a mound covered by weeds and vines. Stuck here so far away from the house with a line of trees and bramble behind it, it would be easy to miss.

"I know it looks like a pile, but it was a shed. We used to dare each other to go in it."

"Afraid of ghosts?"

"No," she said, a fond look on her face. "Spiders and mice. We were so young…"

I left her to her reminiscing and did one circle of the junk heap. On closer inspection, there was more than just an old shed here.

Beer bottles, bags of garbage, old boxes, buckets, and a sink split cleanly into four pieces—all green with moss and age—poked up out of the pile, proving this had been used as a dumping place for some years now.

"You've seen the journal?" I asked, my hands on my hips, as I tried to decide how to navigate the mess. If I had hands, human hands, I'd be able to dig my way into it. But as an Unliving, there were limitations to how much I could actually affect the living world.

It was not easy for me to physically move physical objects.

I could do it. I'd spent years practicing and getting good at it. But practice or not, it always took a lot of focus and energy and will. And those things were easily depleted.

Death took its toll, and so did almost-death.

"It was there. I know it was there," she said.

"What you're saying is you haven't seen it."

She drew herself up. "I left it there. I haven't seen it, but I *know* it's there. Can't you feel it?"

Truth was, I hadn't tried. I was good at finding magical things. Good enough Lu had made a living trading in trinkets and tricks and antiquities for years.

Good enough she supplied Mr. Headwaters who trusted her eye and would pay half again above any other bidder when Lu put something magical up for auction.

He had remained a mystery to the both of us, having only sent messages via delivery services and, more recently, texts.

But looking for magic, opening up for it, well, that took energy, focus, and will too.

Spend a penny, lose a pound. I didn't want to exhaust myself. I needed to talk to Lu tonight.

I stared at the pile, wishing the journal would bubble up like some kind of leaf knocked free in a storm gutter. But since that wasn't happening, I cleared my mind, took a deep breath, and *felt*.

It was like stretching my arm out into a dark hallway and feeling my way forward as I took small steps. I was blind—this had nothing to do with my eyes, but still, it felt like I couldn't see. Like I was surrounded by darkness.

Breathe out.

My senses exploded.

Magic is everywhere in our world. There's not a single stone, plant, or person who doesn't have at least a little of it on them. Like a fine dust, magic sticks to things. Some things and people, it sticks to a bit more. Or sometimes a thing or person can be in a place where the magic is so thick, it covers them in thicker and thicker layers. Maybe they breathe some of it in, maybe they swallow some of it down.

Maybe it becomes a part of their blood, their sweat, their tears.

Then they carry that magic around and they spread it, leaving little bits of it on the things they touch, or in the people they love.

I didn't believe in magic when I was alive. But now that I was dead, I wondered how I'd ever ignored it.

I could smell it: sweet apples and the hot spice of cloves, the sharp sap of broken sticks and crushed grasses. I could taste it on my tongue, at the back of my throat, and I swallowed it down as easy as warmed wine that spread through me with a soft wash of pleasure.

I could hear it, a song of bells, chimes caught in a distant wind, horns calling, a hushing burble of a stream.

It was *here, here, here,* calling, reaching, clinging, drawing me in, as if I were made of infinitely small grains of sand, and magic was a tide pulling me apart, piece by piece, out into the depths of the sea. Pulling me home.

I opened my eyes to a changed world.

Magic was *everywhere.* It flowed in streaming pastel rivers over the earth, down the trees, around the rocks. It glowed out from under the heap of junk that had once been a shed. Whatever was in there, I assumed the magic journal, pulsed with the blinding white of powerful, bound magic.

Dangerous magic.

"Can you… Do you feel it?" Stella asked again.

"Yeah," I said, that hot white magic buzzing like lightning across my lips. "I can feel it."

Stella looked different too. Less of a ghost and more like the living woman she had been.

No longer drifty and translucent, she cut a solid figure. Her hair was tied up in a bun and loose strands fell free, a few sticking to the side of her face in soft curls. Her eyes were brighter—hazel like Dot's—and I caught the hint of the flowery Avon perfume she must have worn in life.

"Can you reach it?" she asked.

I stepped up to the edge of the pile, crouched down, and shoved my hand into the ruins. My hand passed through all the solid bits easily enough, then my arm, shoulder, and head. The harsh light of that concentrated magic stung my eyes and made it hard to breathe.

Whatever was down there, it was hellishly powerful. Stronger than anything else we'd dug up over the years.

I wondered how it had stayed buried this long. Surely someone or some*thing* should have found it by now.

I stretched a little more, holding my breath as I reached.

My fingers brushed the edges of something smooth and flat. A book. I was sure it was a book.

Then lightning shot out of the sky—

—*hot hot agony*—

—pounding me into the ground like a two-ton hammer.

CHAPTER TEN

The dream was always the same.

"What about today?" Lu asked, helping me upend the chairs and stack them on the tables.

The bakery, which was now also a soup and sandwich shop, had been closed for an hour. It belonged to her family. It had fallen to Lu to run, now that her dad had passed. It was 1936 and Lula Doyle was a modern woman with dreams of growing her business.

She had lived in Chicago all her life. I'd only arrived a few years ago, on my own since my parents died and us siblings scattered rather than get thrown into orphanages.

I'd made it through the last year of high school here, working the rail line, farms, shipyards, and any other job I could find.

I slept in a broken shack on the outskirts of town with more holes than walls. It was enough for now, but wasn't where I planned to live for long. I'd been saving up for a future. I was a modern man with dreams too.

But work was scarce, and they said that wasn't going to

change now that the country was depressed. Every headline assured us all it was only going to get worse.

I'd tried to get work in a library, a radio station, or with the government. I had the grades and the brains for any of those, but as soon as anyone got a look at me—built bigger than an ox—the only jobs they thought I'd be suitable for involved swinging some kind of hammer.

Not that I was complaining. I had health, youth, and grit. I could weather any storm.

Especially if Lula Doyle was in my life.

"Where's your head, Brogan?" She sashayed behind me and flicked the towel off her shoulder, smacking me in the arm with it. "I thought you liked working here."

"Oh, I do," I said fast, because I didn't ever want her to think I didn't want to be with her. I didn't ever want her to think I didn't want her.

"Then work."

I hoisted a chair in each hand and settled them on the table with ease.

"And answer my question," she said.

"If we should get married now?" I tried to say it casually. As if this one thought wasn't taking up all the room left in my brain. As if it wasn't eating all my reason out of house and home.

"The courthouse is open for another fifteen minutes," she said, and maybe she was trying to hide the excitement in her words. But I knew her. Better than I knew anything else in the world. I could hear her hope, giving each word shine. "I've got the fee saved back."

I scowled at her. "No, I've got the fee saved back. I'm not going to let you pay the judge. I told you, if we go to the courthouse, I'll pay the fee."

"So let's do it!" She spun and her hair spun with her, tied back in a band, but still long enough to brush along her back and shoulders like flame bending in the breeze. She was fire, this woman, and I couldn't wait to warm myself to her for the rest of my life.

"I thought…you know, we have almost enough to hire a preacher. Almost enough for cake and lemonade. We could have it here, right here in your shop. Or out back, under the big ash tree."

"You want a wedding." She wasn't asking a question because she already knew the answer.

"Yes. I want a wedding. More than just a courthouse and a judge. I want…"

How did I tell her this? That I'd dreamed of it, hoped for it, ever since I first put my eyes on her. There would be flowers and cake and maybe even ribbons. She'd wear a dress, and I'd have a suit and top hat. And we'd join hands and hearts and lives right there in front of people who cared about us.

She would smile and that would be my world. My whole world in her smile.

"I want everything. For you. For us." I closed the distance between us and took both of her hands in my own. "If you can be patient. Just wait a little more. I know I'll have enough money."

"We'll have enough money," she corrected. "We are both saving. We could both pay for it. Together."

"All right. Yeah. I like that. If we wait." I pulled on her hands, bringing her even closer to me. She tipped her head up, that quirk of a smile telling me she'd gotten what she wanted.

"You'll wait?" I said. "For me to get everything arranged?"

"For you," she said, and her voice was honey and spring and sun on my skin, "I'd wait forever."

I raised one hand to cup the side of her face and bent toward her, slow, slow, slow, so I could savor this, being here, being hers.

She lifted, her whole body flowing like a chorus through a choir, and I was her audience, mesmerized by every movement. I dragged my thumb gently across her lower lip as she smiled, amazed once again that she was mine. That I would know her, touch her, love her for the rest of my life. It was a gift I never thought I'd be given, and one I didn't think someone as poor as me could ever earn.

"Kiss me?" she whispered.

"Always," I answered.

Her eyes were green and bright and oh, how I burned as I gently pressed my lips to hers. Briefly. So foolishly briefly.

I woke, cold and shivering, frozen in the night. Alone. The sky hung spangled with stars, a breeze hushing leaves and grasses around me. A slug slowly pushed its way through my ankle, unfazed by my presence.

The moon was up, full and heavy, nearly at the height of the sky. Time had passed. Hours.

I bent knees, planted my boots, and sat, holding still as my head swam and the world rocked. Whatever kind of magic had hit me, it had done damage. I felt like I'd been tied to a barbed wire fence and electrocuted.

The shed was a good twenty feet away, Stella was nowhere to be seen, and the glow of magic from the buried journal still shone out of the junk pile like a headlight stuck on high beam.

"All right," I grunted as I stood. "Plan B." I ached from my heels to my molars. I didn't dare touch the buried journal again. Not until I knew what kind of magic bound it.

I pressed the heels of my hands against my eyes and waited out another dizzy spell. A small vibration, light as a moth's wing, fluttered in the center of my chest.

Lu was waiting for me.

Our soul connection was strong. There wasn't a place on this earth where I couldn't find her. But the farther away from the Route either of us traveled, the harder it was to feel each other and the longer it would take me to track her down.

East. She was east.

I traveled toward the pull of our connection, passing through the world, across the flat land faster than any living thing. Houses, trees, fields, and more fields slid by so quickly, they were a ghostly blur.

Then I was there. In the graveyard, the moon slanting down through the branches of an old white oak tree, neat rows of sparse gravestones stippling off to either side of me. Lu was right there, right in front of me, sitting on a curved white headstone.

"Hey," she said, her gaze searching for me and missing by just a few inches. "You're late."

I huffed a laugh and stepped to one side so I could pretend she could see me. "I'll tell you all about it," I said. "One minute, love. Let's do one."

Lu angled her chin up, exposing more of her pale neck to moonlight. The dull glimmer of the chain around her throat caught my eye, and I followed the links down to the pocket watch hidden beneath her shirt.

She inhaled, exhaled. I watched as her shoulders settled and her heartbeat picked up. She was excited, afraid, hungry.

I was all those things too.

She ran her finger along the chain and pulled the watch free. "One minute," she said.

She cupped the watch in her palm, exhaled through her mouth, then pressed the stem with her thumb.

It was strange, this magic. We'd never found any other like it in the world. It snapped hot, a violent, phosphorus flame suddenly alive, surrounding the watch, eerie in the shifting colors of amber, blood.

The flame was not hot. It was an arctic wind, so cold, Lu quickly shifted her hold to the chain, suspending the watch away from her skin, even as prickles of goosebumps pebbled her chest.

"Brogan?" she asked, looking for me, waiting for me, for this, our shared sixty seconds.

I wrapped my hand around that watch, shocked as ice pumped through my veins, the endless cold of this magic.

Then...and then I was there, alive—nearly so, as close as I'd ever been able to be.

I saw the moment I became substantial in her eyes, saw the moment she could really see me.

And oh, how she smiled.

"I love you, Lula." It was always the first thing I said. And I knew it would be the last whenever that day finally came.

"I love you, Brogan," she replied.

Before she could say more I immediately bent and

met her mouth with my own, hungry for her touch, aching to feel her in my arms, alive.

I straddled her legs as she stood up into me, pressing full body, as if we could become one person, as if we would never have a chance to feel each other again.

I locked one arm across her back, holding her slighter frame against the massive bulk of me, every curve and edge of her absolutely necessary for me to savor. Her free hand dug up the back of my neck, catching the curl of my hair and tugging hard enough it stung.

Yes.

The kiss grew deeper. I dragged my tongue across her lips gaining easy entrance as her lips parted hungrily for me. She pulled me in, her tongue stroking mine, setting off a fire that spread hot and wild across my chest, pouring like heated oil down my stomach to my groin.

I was on fire.

I groaned. She bit my lower lip and tugged until I growled.

She released my lip, then licked across it, soft nips and kisses soothing the pleasurable bruising she'd marked me with.

I wanted more. So much more. I wanted to carry every touch and bruise and nip. To remind me I was alive. To remind me she was mine, I was hers. Even if only for one spare minute.

"The truck," I said, unable to stop kissing her, fitting my words between each taste.

"You like it. It's silver," she said.

"It's a piece of junk."

She pulled back, eyes wide. Her pupils were completely blown, the honey gold nearly eclipsed by the center of black. Her lips, wet and red and a little puffy, would carry the mark of our kiss, and I felt a deep satisfaction at that settle heavy in my stomach.

She was beautiful, wild, alive, and it took everything I had not to pick her up and lay her on this cool, moonlit ground and make her never forget she was mine.

"It's silver—your favorite color—has almost no miles on it, and as soon as Calvin is done fixing it, it's going to be amazing."

"You can't help but fall in love with lost causes, can you?"

"There's only one thing I love in my life, and he's not a lost cause. Not even close."

"That thing better not be the truck," I growled.

I shifted my hold and dragged my hand up her back, burying my fingers in her long, silky hair. I tugged gently, urging her to tip her head. She shivered.

"You like the truck," she repeated, chin raised.

"Maybe I just like the woman who likes the truck."

"That works too."

"The hunter checked into the Super 8," I said. "He has a gun. And explosives."

"If he wanted to kill me, he has had his chance."

"He wants something here," I said.

"Dot?" she suggested.

It was a reasonable guess, since he'd tried to check into the B&B.

"There's a journal under the junk pile in the back-yard of the B&B. Stella led me to it, in exchange for a favor."

"Stella?" She scowled and anger triggered flare-gun flashes in her eyes.

I tucked away that look of jealousy for later, when I could savor it, chuckle about it, add it to the ever-thinning lifeline of moments we shared. Still, my chest puffed up, even as I rubbed my thumbs gently below her eyes and bent so our gazes met.

"The ghost from the bedroom. Dot's sister. Sits in the corner chair and knits. She wants to talk to Dot. Personally. Price for the journal. They used to dare each other to go in the shed. She was afraid of the spiders. Man at a fair tried to sell her the book. Oh, and she died in a car accident."

The emotions raced across her face almost faster than I could catch. We'd gotten good at this, at saying so much more, at saying everything in seconds. Because that was all we had left to us, seconds of time on a watch wound with magic we could not understand nor tame.

"Fifteen seconds," she said. She didn't have to look at the watch to know. We could feel it, the darkness closing in at the corners of our vision, eating all light, eating the reality of the world around us.

And with it came pain. It began, even now, with cold shocks, like hailstones falling on every inch of our skin, hitting hard enough to leave welts. They'd turn to icicles soon, then knives, swords, until the pain was so harsh, so cruel, we'd both be left bleeding and broken.

We'd tried to wait it out the first time. Had held

hands for exactly a minute and ten seconds. When I woke a day later, Lu was still unconscious, and it had taken her a week to walk. A month for all the bruises and swelling to fade.

I'd sworn never again. And even though it was the hardest thing in my life to resist, we had never done it again.

This…this was what was left to us. One minute at a time. And that only sparingly. Once a week we could endure. Better only once a month. But we'd found meeting in a graveyard made it easier, staying near the route helped, too, and if the moon was out, that was three pluses in our favor.

"I tried to reach the journal, and the magic blasted me on my rump. I blacked out. I'm fine, Lu, love, I'm fine."

But she kissed me, nodding as she did so, telling me more, telling me everything as our seconds counted down.

"Be careful with the journal," I said, knowing she'd find a way to retrieve it. "If the hunter's smart, that might be what he's after."

"I'll talk to Dot. Stella can talk to me."

"She wants it personal." I hated this, what I was asking her. To allow another person, another soul, to step into her body and exist there, under her skin, seeing her memories, her fears, her joys, and her shame.

Jealousy and hot anger burned steady inside me, but that would have to wait. I had had years and years to get used to being angry about this curse. Years to rail against every thing and person who could touch Lu, laugh with her, talk to her, know her.

Jealousy was an old friend.

"I can do it," she said. "It's fine. Just let me know what the trick is to get the journal. If it's that strong, I can get half a year's wages out of Headwaters."

"Five," I said. Five seconds. "I love you."

"I love you."

Then we kissed, soft and slow, need and desire, a promise. The same promise we always made. This wasn't the last time. We would touch each other again. We would have each other again.

For more than a minute.

For a lifetime.

Until our last breaths.

The cold stabbed, ice cracking my skin, biting at my bones. But her lips were the sun, her body the world, and I held her until the final second fell away.

Lu's thumb, my thumb over it, pressed down on the pocket watch's stem.

Just like that, my arms were empty, even though Lu was still there, her arms around me, her breathing carefully steady, as if she were fighting not to scream. A single tear glinted on her cheek, diamond bright in the moonlight. I brushed it away, but my thumb was insubstantial, ghostly, nothing.

I forced myself to step backward, my hands dropping away from the woman I loved.

"I love you, Lula Gauge."

"I love you," she whispered, her eyes finding me,

holding mine with that fierce light. It was a promise, a threat. She wasn't giving up on us. I wasn't allowed to give up on us either.

As if I ever could.

CHAPTER ELEVEN

Sunshine's shop was busier than I expected for a Saturday. He got rid of Doug's car and sent Doug himself packing.

Doug was furious and said he'd never use Fisher's Auto again. Sunshine told him that was the idea.

Four other vehicles arrived for a variety of maintenance and repair.

Sunshine was pleased with the business, though he kept glancing out the front windows as if he were expecting someone.

That someone was Jo. She'd left right before dawn to get the new modem and other equipment from the main office in Springfield. She hadn't returned yet.

But it wasn't Sunshine, his employees, or the stream of customers I was paying attention to.

It was Lu.

She hadn't slept when she had returned to her room. She'd stretched out on one side of the bed, leaving the other open for me. I'd curled there, the bed almost too short for my height, my elbow bent and head propped on my fist, watching her.

She faced me and rubbed her palm slowly back and forth across the sheets that were expensive and therefore very soft.

All the while, her eyes searched for me.

I finally pressed my palm over the back of her hand. "Rest, Lu. It's going to be a long day tomorrow."

Her hand stalled, and she turned it over, palm up. "The truck's going to be ready tomorrow."

"I know," I said, even though she couldn't hear me.

"I'll get the journal. I'll call Headwaters."

"Yeah."

"There's a good custom shop in Oklahoma," she said.

"Ruck's Trucks," I agreed. "'Course there's a good custom shop in every state."

"I think I should head to the coast. Talk to Marty."

"Marty tried to shoot you last time you showed up, Lu," I said, wishing I could feel the heat of her hand. "He doesn't like monsters like you and me."

"He's coming around, I think."

I snorted. "Not likely."

"He has information. I know he does."

"Here we go again."

"He knows where the gods vacation. Some place in Oregon, I think."

"No. This is a road we promised we'd never walk. Tangling up with gods only gets you deeper into the mess of god egos and god trickery."

"One of them might help us," she said. "It's been years since…since that other one."

That other one was Mithra, a god of contracts who almost got us killed—permanently, violently, and painfully. I'd learned right then and there that gods were something to be avoided, even the minor ones like Mithra.

"We're not going to ask gods for help, Lu. We tried that."

"If we had leverage…something the god wanted… we could make it work."

"No."

"There might be something we've tucked away in the storage unit."

"Oh, hell, no. We worked hard for that, Lu. For all of it. We're not going to trade away a single book or scroll for the favors of a damn god."

"Language, Brogan." She grinned, and I laughed.

"We'll talk about this later," I said.

"I'm going to win this. Find the god's vacation town. Find one who has answers for us," she informed me.

"Well, you're going to need your rest, because I'm going to do everything in my power to make sure you fail. No gods. We don't need that kind of trouble."

She *hmmm*ed, and I felt the warmth in my chest where my heart used to be, where my blood used to be.

"Go to sleep, love," I murmured, wanting to see her rest. Wanting to see the lines across her forehead ease, the tightness at her eyes smooth out. I loved it when she slept. It seemed like the only time she wasn't sad.

She shut her eyes, her hand still stretched out toward

me, my palm over hers. From the rhythm of her breathing, I knew she didn't sleep. Neither did I, but it was good. Good to be there with her.

Until Sunshine called, saying the truck would be up and road ready by the next evening.

Which is why I was leaning on the wall in the garage, watching as Sunshine worked on the underbody of the truck he'd put on the lift, a clean rag hanging out of his back pocket, the short-sleeved, blue shirt with his name over the pocket tucked into a pair of worn, but clean jeans.

Lu was there, too, in the garage where a radio played a mix of rock and country, watching him work. "Jo left early this morning," she said.

Sunshine ducked out from under the vehicle, his hand still stuck up in the guts of its underbelly. "Did you see her?"

"Yes."

"Was she...Did it look like she was coming back?"

Lu tipped her head and studied him for a minute. Then every line of her softened, and I groaned.

"He is not adorable," I said.

"I think that was the plan." There was humor in Lu's voice. And fondness.

"They can fall in love on their own, Lu," I grumbled.

"Did she say anything?" He pulled out the rag, crumpled it in his free hand, then realized he didn't need it and stuck it back in his pocket again.

"She said she was leaving early so she'd get back in time for lunch with you."

He dropped the wrench. It gave a harsh ring as it hit the concrete floor.

I shook my head and stared at the sky. "Lost cause. Just can't let it be, can you, babe?" I crossed my arms, then glanced at Lorde who was lying at my feet, her big fuzzy head resting on her outstretched front paws.

"Tell her to stop trying to get these two perfectly capable *adults* to fall in love."

Lorde wagged her tail, but didn't look up from her paws, didn't open her eyes.

Lu glanced over, though, and flashed a small smile. A smile just for me.

"Lunch with me?" he repeated. "She said that?"

"She said in time for lunch. I assumed you'd want to join her."

"I do. Yeah." His hand drifted back to the cloth in his pocket, but instead he lifted his empty hand to rub the back of his neck. "You think she…Did she give you any indication that she, um, she might like me?"

The slashes of red across his tanned face were a dead giveaway of just how much he wanted Lu's answer to be yes.

Lu walked over to him, bent, and picked up the dropped wrench. "I think it's early, but yes. I think she might like you."

She held out the wrench, and he grinned, a flash of white teeth and joy, then he reined it in, nodding and nodding. The red still stained his cheeks and washed down the back of his neck. I could sense his heartbeat and it was galloping a mile a minute.

"Easy, Romeo," I said. "Just because she likes you doesn't mean she's staying. In this town?" I snorted.

And just like that, the smile fell off his face and his color went flat. "She's never going to want to stay here. This town?"

Lu's eyebrows went up at his sudden change of mood. She turned and glared in my general area.

I shrugged. "Not my fault he heard me."

Lu gave me one slow, warning blink.

"Yeah, yeah," I chuckled. "I'll shut up, so you can meddle in other people's lives. This truck cannot be finished quick enough for me. Right, Lorde?"

The dog gave a soft, sleepy *woof* of agreement.

"At least one of you are on my side."

Lu was ignoring me completely now, her stance square. She was going to talk sense into this young man until he wised up and asked Jo out on a date. Or asked her to marry him, or live with him, or whatever plan she was set upon.

"I think you're doing an awful lot of deciding things for her," Lu said in a clear, reasonable tone. Like a school teacher who was a little disappointed a student hadn't given his A+ effort on an assignment.

"And I think you should stop assuming things about her, and asking me things you should be asking her."

Sunshine's head shot up. He couldn't have looked more surprised if a yeti had strolled into the shop looking for a snow mobile repair.

"Ask her if she'd like to go on a date," Lu went on. "Ask her if you can try a long distance thing. Ask her if she'd consider staying in McLean for awhile as a home base for her road work. Ask her if she could come to like living in a small town. Ask her if you can visit her at her place. Ask her. All of that. Any of that."

He was staring at his boots now, the rag in his hand along with the wrench, worry and hope wrestling his face into interesting expressions.

"Yeah," he finally breathed. "I should. You're right. I should. So...lunch?" He glanced up, a sparkle in his eyes.

"That's what she said."

"Thanks," he said. "I'm not usually..."

"...stupid?" I asked.

"...so caught up about someone. I mean, I've dated, but when I saw her. Even from that first minute, it was like..." His voice faded out, his eyes got distant, and I knew he was seeing her, seeing that moment again, like it was water in a desert, gifts on Christmas, and puppies in bows all in one.

"All right, all right," I grunted. "You win, Lu. He's got feelings for her. Maybe not love at first sight, but it's at least like at first fight."

"Do you think someone can fall in love at first sight? Even if he's been an awkward clod?" Sunshine asked.

She nodded. "Absolutely. Even awkward clods can be pretty charming. I know a few."

Yeah, I knew that was for me. I chuckled. "Fine. Fine. I give up. You just stir this pot and mess with these poor people's lives. I'm sure it won't blow up in your face."

Lorde gave another soft *woof*.

"Hey, Cal!" A man strode into the garage like he

lived there. The other employees looked up from their work long enough to wave.

Sunshine nodded toward the newcomer.

Lu turned so her back wasn't to the man, though I knew she would have heard him coming for some time now.

I watched the man too. He was just a little taller than Sunshine, his hair a little darker, and his clothes more business casual—a plaid button-down and clay-colored chinos. But the rest of him bore a sturdy resemblance to Calvin.

Brother? Cousin? Maybe uncle?

"Keith," Sunshine said. "This is Lu Gauge. Lu, my brother, Keith Fisher."

Keith offered his hand, with a "Nice to meet you," and Lu shook it.

Lorde hopped up onto her feet and jogged over to Lu. The dog shook her head, making the tags on her collar jingle. It was her signal for wanting to go outside.

"When should I check back?" Lu asked Sunshine.

He glanced at the truck as if he could read a timer attached to it. "I'd say a couple hours? If you want, I can call and let you know when it's done."

"No need," Lu said as she made her way to the shop door. "I'll stop in later."

She walked outside with Lorde at her side. I lingered, watching the men.

"What brings you by?" Sunshine asked.

"Do I need an excuse to see my baby brother?"

"I'm not fixing your refrigerator, snaking your drain, or hanging your gutters."

Keith grinned, and the resemblance was impossible to miss. "Would I ask you to do such a thing?"

"You asked me to do all those things."

"I paid you for your time."

"Pizza and beer doesn't cover rent, bro."

Keith laughed. "Well, this isn't for me this time. Mom wants to pull up the carpet and have the floors redone. I thought we could save her the labor."

"She's gonna try to do it on her own?"

"Of course."

Sunshine sighed. "Yeah, of course she is. When do we start?"

"I can keep a hammer out of her hands until maybe Friday."

"How are you going to pull off that miracle?"

"I'll tell her the Dumpster isn't available for renting until then."

Sunshine smiled. "That works. I can make an early day of it."

"Good. Good." He slapped his brother on the arm and turned to leave. But then he thought better of it and half turned back to him.

I heard voices outside. Lu and a woman. Took me a second to recognize the woman was Jo. She sounded happy, excited. Lu was already talking about lunch, and how she should have it with a certain mechanic who was interested in her.

Sunshine was oblivious to the conversation, going over the details of what they'd each need to bring to help with their mom's renovation.

I pushed off the wall and started to walk out to Lu, but something Keith was saying caught my attention.

"She's the tech girl, right? The one with the piercings?"

"Yeah. Her name's Jo. Just..." He leaned in toward his brother, closing the space as if he didn't want his employees hearing what he was about to say.

"...what do you think about her? Really?"

"I've only seen her once, at the gas station. Why?" Keith straightened a little, then a knowing grin spread across his face. "Oh, it's like *that*, is it?"

"Might be. Yeah. I think it is," Sunshine said. "So what do you think about her?"

Keith leaned back to open the space up between them. This wasn't something he thought needed to be private, his opinion, apparently, good enough for public airing.

"I think Jo's...different."

Sunshine scowled. "Different."

"With those tattoos and piercings? That hair? Yeah, she's different. She sure isn't someone from around here, is she? I mean, can you imagine her mucking out a stall or putting up with the crappy internet reception when the storms roll through?"

"I don't—"

"She's just passing through." Keith slapped his brother on the arm again. "But hey, never hurts to sample the flavors before you buy the cone."

Sunshine frowned. "That's not—"

Keith laughed. "Use your brain, bro. She's big city. She's aiming for a...life." He waved his hands to indicate the world at large. "Something a hell of a lot bigger and better than this podunk town. Admit it. The way she is? She's not like us."

Calvin hardened in some way. It was in the set of his jaw, in the angle of his hands and chest.

"Yes. She's…not like us." The way he said it made me pause. It was flat, almost emotionless. As if this was the kind of non-agreeing agreement he'd been doing with his brother for years. A way not to start a fight. A way to keep the peace with someone who always got his own way.

I could hear that in his tone. But I was pretty sure from the look on Jo's face, as she lingered there in the doorway, she couldn't.

Keith strode off with a wave over his shoulder and a "Friday!"

He nodded just slightly to Jo as he passed her in the doorway.

Sunshine saw her and he knew she'd overheard at least some of their conversation.

She shook her head, her hands diving into her pockets as she strolled over to him.

"Not like you, how?"

"It's not…he's my brother. I just…"

"He gets to decide who's good enough for this town?"

"No. You've got it wrong…You're…"

"Do I? Can you imagine me trying to survive crappy internet? I'm just too *different* to survive such a terrible hardship, just don't have what it takes to handle hard things. Not like you special, *normal* people born in McLean."

"You are blowing this out of proportion."

"Or maybe I'm seeing this," she waved one finger at him, then at his shop, and the world beyond, "for what it really is."

"Jo."

"If all you special people do in this town is judge others behind their backs, then I can't wait to get out of here."

That did it. Sunshine went red again. "Why? Because in the city everyone is *nice* to you?"

"I don't expect everyone to be nice to me. But I don't expect someone to judge me behind my back after they've asked me out to lunch. Twice. But hey, I'm *different* that way."

Sunshine shut his mouth. The muscle at the corner of his jaw bulged as he ground down on his back teeth. He crossed his arms over his chest, and his nostrils flared.

His voice, when he spoke, was low and calm. "Maybe this is a bad idea from the start. I'll take my share of the fault in that. But I thought you were different in all the best ways, Jo. Thought you wouldn't judge me by what other people said."

Jo had mimicked his stance, her arms crossed over her chest. She was looking at him like she'd heard this song and dance before and wasn't buying it. Like someone had said these things before and it had been a lie.

"I don't need your approval," she said.

"That's fair. I'll need my computer and internet connection up and running before you go. Please."

She bit at the inside of her bottom lip, looking like she was chewing back a yelling spree. I could tell she'd been burned by people before. Could tell she had learned not to trust.

"Fine," she said.

He nodded and turned his attention back to the truck, hands busy with the wrench.

The music of the garage seemed to fill the room again. It was a slow sad song about somebody doing somebody wrong that I hadn't heard in awhile.

The employees who had all worked a little slower, a little quieter so they could hear every word of the argument, kicked it back into high gear, suddenly busy and running noisy equipment.

"If he's not willing to stand up for you to his brother," I said to Jo, "maybe he's not worth your trust. Maybe you should just let it go."

She frowned, standing there for an extra moment or two, as if the thought of that didn't make her happy at all. Then she turned and strode out of the garage to the office.

Sunshine dropped his hands at his sides and couldn't help himself. He watched her go.

I groaned. Lu was right. These two had feelings for each other.

"That did not go well for you," I said. "You could just set down your wounded pride at being misunderstood, and tell her you like her. Tell her your brother is a jerk, but he's not you. I think she'd listen."

The door to the office slammed loud enough it echoed like a gunshot through the garage.

"Never mind," I said. "I think this ship has cut anchor and sailed."

Sunshine blinked hard, like his eyes hurt, exhaled, and got back to work.

CHAPTER TWELVE

I caught up with Lu. She was a couple streets over, headed to Dot's place.

"It didn't go well," I said, as I fell into step next to her.

"Day's not over yet," she muttered.

I knew she'd heard the argument, or if not that, the door slamming. And there was no mistaking who had slammed that door.

"You romantic, you. You never give up." I reached over and dragged my fingers gently across the back of her hand. She tipped it open so I could press my palm to hers.

"I'm going to look for the journal," she said. "Then I'll talk to Dot about her sister. Unless you have another idea?" She angled her head as if she could hear my voice in the wind, her eyes dropping to Lorde.

Lorde looked up at her, then at me. When I said nothing, Lorde just went back to walking a few steps ahead of Lu, stopping to sniff random weeds growing out of the sidewalk.

"Okay," Lu said. "Let's see what we can do."

She picked up the pace and in short time was rounding the house to the junk pile in the back. She approached it warily, her hands loose at her sides as she walked a slow circle around the edge of the old shed.

I stood to one side of the pile, waiting for her to decide how she was going to do this. It was the middle of the day and sunny. Anyone who happened by would see her digging. But there were no roads back here, just yard and trees that abutted more yard and trees.

"I'm sorry I didn't warn you," Stella said.

I turned at the sudden appearance of the ghost.

"Warn me about what?"

"That the journal might knock you out."

"You knew that was going to happen?"

She shook her head as she watched Lu assess the situation. "I thought it might. It's very strong magic. The man I stole it from said it could only be owned by a person it chose."

I didn't like the sound of that.

"So it chose you?"

She shrugged. "He was selling it. For all I know he just said that so I would want it more. If so, it worked."

"Enough you stole it."

"To have something magic choose you," she went on, as if I hadn't spoken, "proving you're different, and worth something. I guess I wanted that." She sighed. "I really wanted that."

This woman, born and raised in this very small town

had yearned to be different. I reflected on Sunshine and Jo's argument and couldn't get over how it had gone bad very quickly over a small matter. A misunderstanding on difference.

Was being different bad?

I thought Jo, like Stella, liked being different. It was reflected in her piercings, her style. It was reflected in this job she'd chosen, being on the road, meeting new people and places.

I didn't think Jo thought being different was bad. But when someone assumed different was instantly wrong, well, that was a problem.

As for Sunshine, I thought he might have been blindsided at having strong feelings for a stranger in so short a time. Afraid of what he might suddenly want and how vulnerable that might make him feel.

I could see how it might shake up both of them.

"Did you use it?" I asked Stella. "The journal? Did you use any of the magic?"

She stared at me for a minute, then, seeming to make up her mind, spoke. "Once. About a year before I died. I used it to make a wish. Or, I don't know, maybe it was a blessing. For Dot. I wanted her happy. To find someone. To have the life she wanted."

A cold chill raced down my skin. Magic used is magic paid for. If she'd been careless, it would be easy for magic to take her life to pay for Dot's happiness.

"She's had a good life, don't you think?" I said, offering her the comfort of not telling her the full truth. "Kids, husband, inherited this pretty old house and is making a profit sharing it with people."

"Yes," she said hesitantly, then a little stronger, "yes, she has. I mean sometimes I thought my…my accident would ruin it all for her. But she's okay. She's doing good. I just want her to know…to know I don't blame her for what happened."

"The accident?"

She nodded and pressed her lips together, as if it took a physical effort to keep the words inside.

"Lu said she'll do it. Let you talk to Dot."

The smile lit Stella's face until she practically glowed. I could see the younger woman in her, could imagine how she would have laughed.

"I know it might be hard…" she said.

"…will be hard," I corrected. "This is going to hurt both of you." After a second, I added: "Maybe hurt all three of you. Dot has thought you were dead and gone for years now. Knowing you've been here all this time might be hard on her."

"Oh. I hadn't thought of that. But I know she'll want to see me. I know she's been thinking all these years that the accident…" She closed her mouth again, her eyes darting up to me like I'd tricked her into talking.

"She'll be fine," she said. "And then I can… Well, whatever comes next, I'll be at peace with it."

I didn't contradict her. Sometimes the best thing you could do for a person was offer them a little grace.

"It's bright," Lu said. "I smell apples and hickory and something sweet. Nectarine? No, roses."

I sniffed the air, but didn't smell anything but a hot Illinois day.

"If there's any reason I shouldn't try to get it out of there," Lu said, "now's your chance to tell me." She waited, and as always, her gaze scanned the area and rested so near where I was standing, the pounding of my heart tripped a beat.

"It's good, love," I said, pushing those words, my encouragement, my concern. "But be careful."

She nodded softly, as if hearing the far off warble of a mourning dove calling its mate. Then she took a deep breath and knelt on top of the fallen bricks, which were covered in moss and dirt.

The shed had been built of sturdy stuff in its day, but Lu was strong. Plenty strong enough on her own to move bricks and wood that should take two people to carry.

Plenty strong enough to push aside rubble and dirt. Plenty strong enough to partially unbury the journal so that it would be easier to reach.

I was so intent on watching her lean forward, one hand extending slowly, as if she were carefully reaching into a burning bonfire, that I didn't notice the hunter.

"Nice and easy now, bitch. I don't want to have to shoot you."

Lu froze. It was not fear that held her motionless, it was the hyper-alert stillness of a predator.

She turned her face his way, watched him walk out from behind the tangle of trees—where we should have seen him, should have sensed him. The concealing magic rolling off him made it obvious he had more than just this trick up his sleeve.

Lorde growled and took several steps forward to put

herself between Lu and the man. The dog's ears were back, and her deep bark gave a hint of her ancestry as a guard dog.

Lu's amber eyes hardened to stone. "Hunter."

"Call off the dog," he said, aiming the gun at Lorde's head.

Lorde barked again, showing strong, sharp teeth.

"To me," Lu commanded.

Lorde stiffened, then reluctantly backed up to stand next to Lu, pressed against her side, both of them crouched as if ready to attack.

"I don't believe I introduced myself." The man's voice had a bit of the snake in it. A bit of the reptile. Coldness coupled with patience. A spider confident in the deadly strength of its web.

"My name's Hatcher, and I work for someone very interested in you. Very interested in the things you find."

The gun in his gloved hand did not waver. It was a Glock, a big thing sure to leave holes large enough to slow Lu down. They might not kill her. Not one or two bullets, but if he unloaded the clip into her at close range, she could bleed out.

If he shot Lorde, the very mortal dog would die instantly.

My heartbeat picked up, fury washing sickly hot, then shockingly cold over me as I stood in front of that gun, inches away from his face.

"Put down the fucking gun." I was loud, and I knew how to throw my anger like a fist.

The hunter's head jerked slightly, and his eyes narrowed. He heard me, or maybe he just felt the cold hatred in my words. Either way, he knew I was right there.

He knew I was going to kill him if I had the chance.

"Even if your companion can influence the physical world," Hatcher went on like he was having a front-porch chat over tea, "I can guarantee this house will be reduced to rubble in exactly five minutes unless I get what I want."

He was not lying, I could tell from his heartbeat.

"You're blowing up the house?" I said.

"He's going to blow up the house?" Stella said. "I have to warn Dot. Dot's in there, Brogan. My sister's in there right now!"

"Go. Go!" I said. Then, "Lu he's not lying."

Lu didn't move, but I knew she heard me. Knew she could probably tell he wasn't lying from the beat of his heart, too, from the steadiness of his hand, from the sharp dilation of his eyes.

"What do you want?" she asked.

"The journal. Go on. Pick it up."

"No," I said. "Don't, Lu. Don't. It's a trap. It has to be."

Lu hadn't moved yet, and I was torn between keeping my eyes on the asshole in front of me and watching the woman I loved behind me.

"I give you the journal, and you just walk away? No hard feelings?" Lu didn't sound afraid at all. She sounded bored. "You know I don't die easy. I don't give a damn about that house, and I don't hand over investments to people who threaten me."

"I know a bullet in the head of that dog will change

your mind."

Again, not lying. He was just shooting the shit, out here on a nice day ready to bury a bullet in my dog's brain, ready to fire off a tight enough cluster to kill my wife—and if not kill her, damage her in a way that could be permanent.

And oh, wasn't that a fear? That Lu wouldn't even earn a clean death, but that she would be caught, maybe in a coma, or some other vegetative state, for eternity.

My stomach rolled and soured as that old fear hit me and hit me hard. I opened my mouth to get enough breath into my lungs, so I wouldn't throw up right there.

There really were things worse than death. We'd both seen them.

"It's just a journal, Lu," I said, turning away from the psycho so I could see her hear me. So I could see her understand me. "We'll find something else for Headwaters. Let him have it. We can take care of him later."

Lu had that stubborn look to her. Like she was going to do the dangerous thing, the savage thing. She wasn't a woman who stood idly by as people told her what to do. She'd lived a very long life cutting her own path through the wild.

"Baby, you need to listen to me," I pleaded. "You really need to listen to me. Let him have the damn journal. We'll find something better. We'll make it square with Headwaters."

I thought she was going to argue with me. Thought that bullheaded side of her was about to get her shot, was about to get Lorde shot too.

If that happened, I was pretty sure Hatcher would

just let the house go up in smoke out of spite. I wasn't sure why he needed Lu to give him the journal. He could just tell her to step away from the junk pile and reach in there himself, but he hadn't yet.

He was cautious. Waiting to see what touching that book of strange magic would do to someone like Lu. Which meant he knew something about the book and what powers it held inside.

Dangerous magics.

Hatcher rubbed his thumb along the grip of the gun, bringing Lu's attention back to it. Back to how he had it pointed at Lorde.

Lorde growled, low and menacing. She wanted to attack. She wanted to protect.

Hatcher started counting. "Five…four…"

"This is not going to end well for you," Lu said like she was judging a poorly designed parachute he was about to jump off a cliff with.

"…three…"

Lu rocked forward, her hand and arm pushing into the pile of junk, through the magic that radiated from the journal, her shoulder sliding between a couple crumbling bricks, then a little farther, until her cheek almost grazed the stone. She wasn't looking downward, couldn't really at this angle.

She was looking at Hatcher.

He had stopped counting, but I knew time was running out. If he really meant to blow up Dot's house, what would keep him from doing it after he got what he wanted? Why wouldn't he take the book, shoot our dog, blow up the house, and try to kill Lu?

"Who are you working for, you piece of shit?" Anger pounded behind my bones like a fist trying to punch its way out of my chest.

Stella flickered at my left. "She's not inside. Not that I can see. I think he kidnapped her. I think he kidnapped her and stole her car to leave it here and make us think she was in there, in the house. She might be dead. Brogan! What if she followed the light? I can't find her, Brogan. I can't find her, can't find her!"

If the hunter heard her, he did not show it. His gaze was steady on Lu, his gun unwavering on Lorde.

I was not physical, not any more. Not in the way that the world defines it. But if I were angry enough—and right now I was burning, an inferno, rage and rage and *rage*—I could tear the world apart.

It would cost me, cost me for days and weeks. Could do permanent damage. That was a price I didn't mind paying.

Stella was screaming and screaming, not words, just pain and loss and madness. She was so loud, I almost didn't hear Lu speak.

"I'm going to enjoy this." Lu quickly—almost too fast for eyes to follow—stood.

And wasn't she a sight? A warrior from myth, her hair catching in the little breath of wind, her eyes so amber they were almost yellow, shining. Shining brighter than any magic, brighter than the sun.

She was fire and fury. Facing down a man who didn't know how little of his life he had left.

I couldn't love her more.

The book in her hand burned with magic that

snapped and arced like ghostly serpents made of fire, electricity and sound: a deep, humming thrum. A maelstrom of magic surrounded the book, a collision of light, darkness, and smells: cinnamon, hot metal, snow scraped across an ancient land.

It was powerful. It might even be deadly, all on its own.

Maybe the man who sold it to Stella had been telling the truth. That the journal chose who possessed it. Maybe that's why it had knocked me on my ass. It hadn't chosen me. Didn't want me.

But looking at Lu, it was clear—very clear—that it had chosen her. She was vengeance. She was a queen carved of wildfire and moonlight, the universe in her fist.

That book held more magic than I'd seen in a long, long time. It glowed brighter and brighter in her grip.

Then she threw the book. Right at the hunter's gun hand.

Stella was screaming and screaming. Words now: "bastard," and "kill you," and "my sister," over and over.

A lot of things happened at once.

Lorde barked, deep and vicious, and jagged away from Lu's side, fast, faster, angling at Hatcher from almost behind him instead of head-on.

The book slammed into Hatcher's hand, knocking it down and wide, the gun somehow still in it. Then his hand was up, quick, as he tracked Lorde, trying to get a shot off.

Stella launched at him, hands curved into claws,

aiming for his eyes, screaming, screaming.

He grunted and scrambled back, his free hand coming up to ward off the ghost whose madness and lust to make this man pay was enough to break through.

I pulled at the energy inside of me. The anger, the fear, the sheer violent boiling *need* to break this world into chunks, grind it to dust in my hands, to shatter it until only Lu and I were left standing. Until it there was nothing holding Lu and I apart. Until we were all there was.

"Lu?" Dot said, her voice high with worry and fear. "What is going on?"

Stella stopped hard. Like a light switch popping, she flickered, fingers scrabbling at the hunter one moment, *pop pop pop*, then suddenly beside her sister.

"Dot, oh, Dot," she heaved, tears so close on the heels of terror and relief. "I thought... I thought..."

Stella had moved fast, but so had Lu.

Hatcher wasn't looking at my wife, his eyes tracking the dog who was on him, jumping, jaws open, sharp teeth snapping, blood-curdling snarls of *death* and *blood* and *pain* filling the air.

"No!" I yelled.

Just as Dot screamed.

Hatcher fired. Steady hand. Straight shot. True and terrible.

Lorde barked, a harsh pain-filled yelp. She stumbled as her front leg refused to carry her. Blood bloomed, dark in her dark fur, her shoulder going wet with it, far too quickly.

Lu didn't make a sound. She was flash-lightning, a

slice of fire-tipped steel, her body a blade, a weapon, an end. She devoured the distance between them and threw a punch with her entire body and the speed of her run packed behind it.

He knocked back, flat on his back, but rolled quick, that damn gun still in his hand. When he came up in a crouch, far enough out of reach that Lu couldn't instantly hit him, that gun was aimed at Dot.

"I will shoot her."

Lu stilled, her muscles pulling painfully tight in her battle not to hit him again. She had knives on her, and one of them was in her hand, gleaming wickedly bright. There was magic in that knife, magic that did unholy damage to creatures and maybe even gods.

In the right hands, that knife could do unholy damage to anyone.

Lu was the right hands.

Lorde still growled, a high whine behind each exhale. She limped to stand next to Lu, her ears back, her teeth bared. But she was not using her front leg, and the bleeding had not slowed.

I stood in front of Lu, facing the asshole down, just angry enough to do something stupid. Something that would lay me out for months. Something that would take me away from Lu for all that time. Something that would get Lorde killed. She was bleeding hard.

Time was running out. Lorde needed a vet. Now.

"The book," Hatcher said.

"Fuck it," I growled. "Give him the damn book, Lu."

Lu didn't want to. It was evident in every line of her

body. But Lorde was running out of time, and Dot, who had wisely held very still and gone gray and silent, didn't deserve to die over a bit of old magic.

Lu slowly bent, picked up the book that *thrummed* at her touch, something not lost on the hunter, if the widening of his eyes meant anything. With a flick of her wrist, she tossed it at his feet.

"I'll find you," she said in a deadly calm voice. A promise. A threat.

"I'm counting on it." He bent, his eyes never leaving Lu, his gun never straying from perfect aim at Dot's heart. He picked up the book with his gloved hand, then stood.

"Who do you work for?" she asked.

"You don't know him."

"Afraid to give me a name?"

"No," he said as he began walking backward. "You have mine."

"You'll want to say good-bye to anyone you care about," she observed.

"I think I'll wait a bit. See how it goes." Brave. And stupid.

He said a word, old and foul. A spell filled with rotted magic not meant for this world filled the air.

I gagged at the horror of it, my hand over my mouth, my arm shooting out to protect Lu and Lorde behind me, like we were on the highway and about to be hit by a truck veering out of its lane.

Then he was gone. Disappeared. That one-word spell poisoning the leaves and grass so that they curled and singed.

I didn't know what it cost him to use that magic. I didn't know whose favor had allowed him to inflict that onto the world.

Whoever he was tied up with was powerful, dangerous, and foul. Maybe monster. Maybe god. Maybe something worse.

"What just happened?" Dot demanded. "He had a gun. And then he was…he wasn't there anymore. I'm calling the police. Should I call the police?"

I spun, hands lifting to touch Lu, to search her for injuries. Lu stood still for a moment, really just a half second. And her eyes met mine. Determination, anger, and fear.

Then Lorde whined and crumpled to the ground.

Lu dropped next to her and gathered the big, black, furry creature into her arms. She stood, lifting the hundred-pound dog as if she weighed nothing. "Where's the nearest vet?"

"He disappeared." Dot still stared at the empty space where Hatcher had been. "He *disappeared*!" It was finally sinking in, and she was having a hard time matching this new reality with the magic-less one she'd believed in just a few seconds ago.

"Dot," Lu's voice cut hard and sharp, bringing the other woman's full attention back to her. "The nearest vet. Now."

Dot's gaze ticked down to Lorde, who was making a soft high whining sound with every exhale.

"Carter," Dot said, snapping into motion. "Dr. Carter's just a few streets down. Get in my car. I'll drive."

CHAPTER THIRTEEN

"She'll be fine," Dr. Joyce Carter said as she finished making notes on the clipboard in her hand. "Lorde is a very lucky girl you got her here so quickly."

Lu sat on the floor, petting Lorde who was sleeping off the anesthesia. She'd had to have immediate surgery to remove the bullet from her shoulder.

The doctor expected a full recovery, though Lorde's leg was bandaged and splinted. She wouldn't be able to put weight on it for a little while, but knowing she was going to be okay meant everything to Lu.

Meant everything to me too.

"Have you called in the incident to the sheriff?" Dr. Carter asked.

Lu shook her head. "I'm sure he's long gone."

"I know we're a small town, Ms. Gauge, but we don't allow people to shoot pets and get away with it. I'm sure if you could identify the man, the sheriff will do everything he can to make sure he's found and brought up on charges."

"Really?" I said. I was sitting on the floor, too, my hand rubbing over Lorde's soft head, her softest ears, mirroring Lu's movements. "You think the law is going to go all out to take down one asshole who shot a dog? You have more faith in how the sheriff departments spend their resources than I do, lady."

"I'll look into it," Lu lied.

There was no chance Lu was going to drag the authorities into this fight. If she wanted revenge, which I was pretty sure she did, she'd catch up with Hatcher and get it with her own hands.

And there was more than him injuring Lorde at stake. There was the book and the magic it held. There was the fact that he was a hunter of things that go bump in the night and might come back to try to kill Lu or Lorde. There was the fact that he had followed Lu, maybe waiting for her to find something magical. Something like the book.

And there was the fact that he was working for someone. Someone who wanted powerful, old magic.

The smart move would be to let it go. Let him take that weird book to whoever he worked for and never think of it again. The smart move would be to go on with our lives, such as they were, looking for our own clues to our own puzzle. To find a way to be whole and alive again.

But I knew Lu. She wouldn't let this lie. Not when she had a chance at magic that might hold the answers we needed. Or make a hell of a bargaining chip to pry answers out of whoever might have them.

"We'll keep Lorde overnight. You can come get her in the morning," Dr. Carter said.

Lu's hand stopped stroking Lorde's fur. I could see her wanting to argue. Wanting to pick Lorde up and carry her out of there right this moment.

When you've had things you loved taken away from you, it was hard to let go, even when it might be necessary and better for the thing, the person, you loved. You held on tight because you knew things could be whisked away, stolen, taken so quickly, so permanently, it hollowed you out and left you empty and numb.

"I'll look in on her," I told Lu. "The truck isn't even ready yet. She'll be more comfortable here than at the B&B. Let Dr. Carter look after her. She's gonna be fine. I'll make sure she's fine."

Frown lines thumbed a curve between Lu's eyebrows, but she finally nodded.

"I'll be here when you open," Lu said.

Dr. Carter smiled, and it was warm and approving. She could see how much Lu loved Lorde. "We will take very, very good care of her. Do you want to see the kennel area?"

Lu did want to see it, so she walked back with the doctor's assistant, a slender young man named Leon. I stayed with Lorde and told her what a good and brave girl she was and made her promises of bones and soft blankets and grassy fields in which she could hunt fat, slow gophers.

When Lu came back, some of the worry had melted away and her shoulders had lost some of their stiffness.

"Good?" I asked her, giving Lorde one last long stroke. Lorde sighed in her sleep. Content. Happy.

Lu nodded. "She's going to be comfortable." I knew she was talking to me, but Leon answered.

"We'll make sure of it. We keep someone here overnight to make sure she has everything she needs. It's my turn. I'm going to pamper the heck out of this brave girl. Chasing off that jerk trying to steal Dot's car."

His brown eyes were so sincere, his smile so wide, it was impossible to doubt him.

"Thank you," she said.

Dot was waiting out in the lobby, sitting in a chair that let her look out the window and keep an eye on the door to the other rooms at the same time.

"How is she?" Dot stood and smoothed her shirt and pants. She was nervous, her hands trembling. I'd thought she would have left, would have been done with this nonsense, but she'd stuck like glue.

"Good," Lu said. "She'll stay the night. I can pick her up in the morning."

"Oh, that's…that's good news. Very good. I can bring you."

"Not necessary. I'll have the truck."

Dot shook her head. "Please. Let me. I can't believe what that horrible man did. And…" Her voice faded as she was reminded of the other unbelievable things that horrible man had done.

Like stealing a book radiating magic. Like disappearing into thin air. "…and that's that," she said. "I'll bring you tomorrow, and we'll make a nice cozy bed for Lorde in the corner of your room. I think I have a small mattress that will fit nicely."

Lu stared at her, and for once, I wasn't sure what she was thinking.

"That's...kind of you," Lu said, "but I won't be staying that long." Lu walked to the door. Dot was right on her heels following her through.

"But Lorde. She needs time to recover."

"She'll be fine. I'll take care of her."

"Of course," Dot said. "Of course you will. I just want you to know you're welcome. Welcome to stay at no charge until she's better."

Lu nodded, but she was scanning the street, scanning the buildings, the barbershop on the corner, the trees stirring in the warm wind.

"I'm sure he's left by now," Dot said, guessing correctly who Lu was looking for. "I called the Sheriff's office, and they think he's long..."

"What?" Lu asked.

"The Sheriff," Dot said. "I called their office. He had a gun. He shot your poor dog. Someone shouldn't get away with that."

Lu lifted her hands to rub at her eyes but stopped before touching her skin. Her fingers were still sticky with dried blood. She'd tried to wipe it off, but hadn't managed to get it all.

Dot noticed she was staring at her fingers and immediately jumped into mother mode.

"Let's get you a shower and a cup of tea. I have a fresh batch of scones and donuts in the trunk of the car.

BunBun's best. You and I can sit on the porch for a few minutes."

Lu frowned at her.

"Just long enough for tea and a scone," Dot promised. "Please. Let me do something to make staying at my old house better. Please."

Lu sighed. "Tea sounds nice."

I grinned. "Aw, she got through your prickly armor. Look at that, Lu. You just made a friend."

Lu shook her head slightly, as if I were being ridiculous, or maybe as if she were.

Either way, she and Dot got in the car, and I ducked into the back seat. I'd ride over with them, make sure they were okay, then come check on Lorde in a bit.

"Tea does sound nice," I said, wishing I could taste it again, wishing I could feel the heat of a cup in my palms, could smell the sweet flowery steam.

I missed the bakery and the quiet times Lu and I would find together after the shop closed, when we would both sit down for a cup of tea or coffee.

"Sounds very nice," I said.

CHAPTER FOURTEEN

Dot was in full hostess gear, sending Lu off to the shower while tea was brewed and BunBun's best were placed on a wooden platter shaped like an apple.

I walked with Lu into the room. Stella was there, sitting in the corner angrily knitting. She didn't look up at me or Lu as we continued into the bathroom.

Lu turned on the shower, then slowly pulled off her boots, socks, shirt, knives, and tank top. Wearing only a baby blue bra, the pocket watch, and her dark jeans, she tossed every other piece of clothing and the weapons into the corner of the room where they tangled in a pile.

"Messy," I said softly.

She smiled, her fingers pausing on her belt buckle. "I'll clean it up later," she murmured.

These old words between us, long ago shared, repeated, and faded, like all our memories. Handled so often they had softened to a hush.

"No, you won't," I told her. Like I always told her.

"I'll pay you to do laundry," she said. Like she always said.

"What are you going to pay me with?" I angled to stand in front of her, both my hands resting on the curve of her waist.

She paused in our ritual, as if she'd forgotten the words. I dragged my fingertips gently up her bare stomach, goosebumps rising on her skin.

Her fingers slipped down into her front pocket.

But instead of saying the next words, she pulled a key out of her pocket and held it up with a smile. "With this."

The magic dripped off of the key like honey oozing down a vine.

The key was burnished silver, shaped as a crow's feather, the tip of the spine worked into delicate rises and dips to fit a lock. It was as long as her finger, and the honeyed magic swirled around it like clouds shifting across a sunset sky.

"Where did you get that?" I asked, even as the realization sank in.

"It was in the book's spine. There's a lock on the book. And this is the key."

And oh, how she burned, fierce and proud. "He might have the book, but he can't get into it."

I stood there while shock, disbelief, and then relief hit me. I chuffed out a laugh. "He'll know."

She nodded. "He'll figure it out. Or whoever he's taking the book to will figure it out."

"He'll come after you."

"And when he comes for me, I'll be ready. We'll

be ready."

I shook my head. "How did I manage to get a woman like you?"

"This could hold our answer," she said. "That book could be the magic we need. The spells we need. I'm not going to let one random hunter take away the chance we can be together again. I'm not going to let anyone or anything get in the way of me having *you*." That last word caught and broke, her eyes shiny with building tears.

"So," she went on, pushing past the tears, "we're going to hunt the hunter."

I smiled, then leaned forward, my mouth so close to hers, I could feel the heat of her breath, and I knew she could feel the chill of mine. "I love you."

She shivered, goosebumps racing over her skin again, her eyes finding mine and holding there. "I love you too."

After the shower, Lu changed into clothes without blood on them, and Dot made sure Lu sat in the most comfortable chair on the porch with the best view.

The tea was in a chubby little pot with a knitted cozy over it. Two cups sat alongside the apple-shaped platter.

I waited a few minutes to make sure the women were settled in and that nothing else was coming to disturb them, then left the porch and crossed town as quickly as a mostly dead guy could travel, arriving at Lorde's side just a minute after I'd left Lu's.

Lorde's tail tapped as soon as I crouched down to peer into her kennel, but she did not lift her head or open her eyes. True to their word, she was surrounded by blankets. Leon sat at a small desk in the corner, humming while he entered information into the computer.

"You good, girl?" I asked. If her tail, *tap-tap-tap*ping meant anything, she was fine. Still sleepy, but doing well.

"I'll come back and check in on you in a few hours." I reached through the grating, my entire hand and arm passing through the metal like it wasn't even there, and smoothed my hand down her silky fur.

She opened her eyes just a slit.

"It's okay, girl. You get some sleep. I'll look after Lu."

Her eyes closed, and she sighed.

Leon glanced over, studying her in case she did anything else, then went back to the computer.

I gave her one last pat and traveled to the porch.

"Hey, sweetheart," I said as I walked up the steps.

Lu looked up from her cup, searching for me. I stood in front of her, touched her face gently, and she unconsciously tipped her head, as if she were trying to hear the distant call of thunder.

"Lorde's resting. She's fine." I pushed that word, wanting Lu to know that I was watching over Lorde, that I was looking over her too.

Her far-off look sharpened, and she tipped her head down, taking another sip of tea.

Message received.

"That man," Stella said from the doorway of the house. She stood on the porch, her ghostly form half in and half out of the closed door behind her. "That monster. He tried to kill my sister."

I sat on the porch railing. If I'd been alive, the thin wood would have cracked and creaked beneath my weight. Even after all these years, it annoyed me that it didn't.

"He did," I agreed.

Her gaze darted to Dot, who was talking about the peonies she'd planted this year and the bluebells she was hoping to get in the ground next year. She was dreaming of fruit trees, maybe peaches, and Lu nodded along, soaking up the comfort of this moment, of these simple dreams.

"You don't have the book," Stella said.

"No. Not yet, anyway."

"Our deal was you could have the book, and I could talk to my sister. But maybe now...maybe now that's gone." Her hands were at her side, hanging, her shoulders squared. She'd stepped the rest of the way out of the house and looked resolved to follow the rules of our deal. She was resigned to letting go of her chance to talk to her sister one last time.

Resigned to giving up the one thing she had clung to this world for. Resigned to sitting in the corner of the house, knitting, watching her sister grow old, and waiting for her to die.

It was a grim reality for anyone, even a ghost. I was having none of it.

"The deal stands," I said.

Her chin ticked up and her eyes went wide. "But the book..."

"We know who has it. We'll find him. You did your part. You showed us where it was hidden. We'll do our part and get it back. So. You want to talk to your sister?"

Her eyes shone with joy, and she took a step, every line of her body canted forward, as if she had been freezing and had finally spotted a fire.

"Yes! Please, yes, please. What do you need me to do? How can I help?"

I stood and rolled my shoulders. I wanted to turn and walk away. Grab Lu's arm, pick up Lorde, get in that ridiculous silver truck and drive. I wanted to protect Lu from this. Wasn't sure if I'd be able to stand someone else touching her instead of me. Someone else knowing her, if even for a few minutes, more than me.

I unlocked my jaw and rubbed at the tense muscle beneath my ear.

Stella was shining and hopeful, but waiting, chewing on a thumbnail and shooting glances between me and her sister, who was thinking maybe a nice long bed of peppers would do best on the south wall.

"Lu," I said, filling that word with my love, with my presence. She turned her face unerringly my way. I crossed the distance between us and crouched down in front of her.

I was big enough that even though she was sitting in the big old rocking chair, and I was hunkered down, we were eye to eye.

"Hey, love," I said, brushing my fingers along the silky braid she'd worked her hair into after the shower. "Stella needs to talk to Dot." I pressed my fingers on the back of her hand, hard enough, and with enough intention, I knew she'd feel the icy touch.

"Okay," Lu said softly. "Dot, I need to tell you something."

"Certainly," Dot said, putting her tea down on the little table and giving Lu all her attention.

"Your house is haunted," Lu said.

Dot sat there, silent for a good long moment. "How do you know?"

It was a strange answer, neither belief or disbelief.

"Because your sister, Stella, has been talking to my dead husband, Brogan."

Again the moment stretched out. Lu held Dot's gaze steady as a surgeon's knife while Dot did some mental calculations for what she was going to believe was real and what she was going to ignore.

"How do you know my sister was named Stella? Who told you? Calvin? Did he tell you that? About the accident?"

"No," Lu said, gentler now. "Brogan told me. He was...I lost him in an...accident too. And he's still with me."

"In your heart. In your memories," Dot insisted.

"Right there." She pointed at where I was crouched, and I grinned until it hurt.

"He's a short man?"

Lu chopped off a laugh.

"You better say no," I warned her, loving that smile, loving that laugh. "Tell her I'm fully grown. A mountain of a man. In every way." I waggled my eyebrows even though I knew she couldn't see me.

"He's kneeling right now. Because he was trying to get my attention," Lu said.

"You can see him?" Dot's eyes were wider, and her color had gone a little off, her lips pale with a slight green around the edges.

"Not clearly, no. But I know him. I know he's there. And he told me your sister, Stella, has been here, in her old room—where I'm staying, right?—waiting to talk to you."

Dot swallowed. "It's, yes. It's her room. But lots of people know what happened. If she's…If what you're saying is true, I need more. To believe."

"I'm right here," Stella said, moving around to stand in front of her sister. "Dotty, I'm right here. Honey, I'm here."

"What would make you believe?" Lu asked.

Dot picked up her tea, lifted the cup to her lips, then put it down again. Her hands were trembling. "Is this because of that man? Are you trying to make…do this because he was…there was a gun in his hand?"

Lu shook her head, a short choppy movement. "I don't screw around with people's feelings or lives."

"Well, except for meddling when you think people should fall in love," I noted.

"There have been very few, *very* few, people I've told ghosts exist. Even fewer know about Brogan. If you don't want me to speak of this, if you don't want to speak to her, I will drop this like it never happened."

Straight, even, clear. There was no doubting Lu was a woman of her word. She'd leave this conversation in an instant and ignore she had ever spoken the words.

It was frightening just how thoroughly Lu could shut down if she wanted to. She hadn't been like that when we were alive. Sometimes it frightened me. Made me wonder how much this half-life had changed her. Made me wonder if we'd ever be together again, happy again, alive.

"I do," Dot said, "want to talk to her. I don't believe in, well, those things."

"I didn't use to either. A long time ago." There was so much sorrow in those words, even Stella made a small, sad sound.

"I'm right here, love." I rubbed my hands on her knees, then lifted one hand, finger extended and poked the tip of her nose.

She jerked her head back, surprised. Then she rolled her eyes. "Fine. I'm being maudlin. Dot, if you want to talk to Stella, I know she very much wants to talk to you. I can prove it's Stella by telling you the details I know, which aren't much. She likes to sit and knit in the corner of her old room. You two used to play in the old shed out back, and she was afraid of spiders. She died in a car accident, and she once met a man at the fair who sold her that book the gunman wanted.

"I haven't actually talked to her, and can't hear her right now, so I can't ask her any questions to prove she's here."

"Then how am I…How can I talk to her?"

Lu's shoulders stiffened. She didn't like doing this either. Letting a ghost possess her, sharing her feelings, her memories, even for a short time.

"She wants to talk to you. Personally."

"I don't understand. Like a séance?"

"No. She wants to speak to you in her own words.

That's…harder. I'm…I can be a channel. She'll share my body and can use my voice. She'll step into me and talk through me."

Lu shrugged like that was that. No big deal. Just an everyday thing. But when she picked up her tea, her hands clenched the cup like she was trying to soak the heat into her body, into her blood.

"It's okay, baby," I said. "We can do this fast. Stella's going to be very, very calm and ignore your memories and feelings. Aren't you?"

Stella moved to stand behind me, then she knelt, her shoulder against mine. She reached out and rested her hand on mine where it was still on Lu's knee.

"I'll do everything Brogan tells me to do. I won't look at your life, your memories, or your fears. I'll be quick. I promise."

"I'm right here," I told her, weighing my words, imagining a blanket wrapped around Lu's thin shoulders, giving her comfort. Giving her warmth.

Lu knew that. She also felt Stella there, the cold of her touch different than mine. Lu was sensitive enough for that.

But it wasn't Lu we were waiting on. It was Dot.

Lu wisely didn't say anything. Just drank her tea and rocked in the chair and gave Dot time to decide. Time to believe, if she wanted, time to deny if she desired.

Stella and I waited, too, and really, there's nothing more patient than dead people.

The sun had lowered behind the trees, throwing a golden light that made everything look like it'd been dipped in maple syrup.

It was hot, but the wind had been steady all day, lifting sweat before it had time to cool.

The tea was gone by the time Dot finally spoke.

"Let's go in the house. I think I'd rather talk to her in her room, if that's all right with you?"

"That's fine."

"Yes," Stella said. "That would be good. That would be nice." She stood, all her focus on her sister, and followed her like a lost puppy as she entered the house.

I remained with Lu, because that's where I would always choose to be. Beside her.

"This isn't going to be easy," she whispered as she turned her hand over, palm up, waiting for mine.

I pressed my palm into hers. "Stella's nice. She'll make it as easy as it can be. I'll help."

Lu inhaled, then exhaled in a thin stream, readying herself.

"That book better be worth it," she said with a grin quick as a sunbeam in a stormy sky.

"That strange old magic ought to be worth something," I said. "But you promise me you'll tap out if this gets too heavy."

She stood, her hand swinging naturally to her side, and walked across the length of the porch leaving just the right amount of space beside her for me to walk with her.

It was those things, those little things, that kept me fighting when things looked impossible. Her determination to keep me in her life was a gift and an honor, and I was not going to let her down.

"Tell her to be quick. And tell her to start with

letting Dot know it's really her. Have her describe something I don't know that only Dot will know."

"Not my first rodeo." I kissed her on her temple.

"Yeah," she said, "but I remember your first rodeo."

I groaned. "Don't."

"You wore chaps. All those tassels. And that swagger."

I huffed and rubbed my free hand through my hair. I had felt like such a fool. But a buddy had told me he could get me into the rodeo for free. He'd also told me girls loved a cowboy, and since I was a hired ranch hand among other things, I was as close to a cowboy as I needed to be to impress Lula.

He'd supplied the chaps too. But he was smaller than me. Most men were. My ass hung out of those things like a drugstore awning, and half the straps wouldn't buckle down properly over my thighs. "You liked that, huh?"

"Your butt in those things made me want to write poetry. And you know I am the worst poet alive."

"You can't even rhyme when you sing along with the radio," I said.

"There goes my man, all dressed in leather, catching my eye in all sorts of ways."

"Weather. Weather rhymes with leather, Lu."

"If he were a statue, he'd be made of fine glass, and every woman who passed him would stare at his t-*ass*els."

I laughed. "All right. No more poetry. You stink at it."

She wandered through the door and down the hall, a slightly dreamy look in her eyes.

"Stop thinking about my ass," I mumbled.

"I'm not. I'm thinking about your ass."

I chuckled.

Lu paused at the doorway to the room. Dot stood inside, all the way over by the window, staring at the chair in the corner. Stella, unsure of what to do with herself, was standing in front of the chair, clutching her knitting in one hand.

They both looked a little wide-eyed and nervous.

"Is she here?" Dot asked. "Right now?" She wrung her hands, squeezing each finger of her left in her right, rings flashing in the low light.

Lu walked over to the bed and sat near the head, tucking her feet up under her. She glanced over at the chair, then back at Dot. "She's here."

"And, how does she look?" Dot's pale skin went rosy. "I mean, obviously she's… um…not alive, but is she, is she okay?"

"Are you okay, Stella?" Lu asked.

Stella glanced at me.

"I'll make sure she hears it," I said.

"Tell her I'm peachy." Stella smiled. "Just like that."

I leaned against the doorway. "She said she's peachy." I put focus and power into it, and Lu nodded.

"Peachy," Lu said.

Dot's mouth dropped open, then she pressed her fingertips over her lips and nodded and nodded.

"Good," she finally said around her fingers, emotion thick in her voice. "Oh, that's so good. Tell her I miss her. Terribly. Every day. Tell her my daughter has her name as a middle name and she hates it." Dot huffed out a laugh, and Stella did the same.

"I never liked it either," Stella admitted.

"This is the hard part," Lu said, pressing her shoulders against the headboard of the bed. "I'm going to let her step into me for about a minute. I know that's short, very short, but any longer will be hard on me and on her."

"It won't be hard on me," Stella said.

"It will," I corrected. "Lu isn't exactly human any more. She's…Well, death and her aren't on good terms, but they're familiar. Stepping into her physical space and mind can be hard on someone like you."

Stella frowned. "Like me? A sister?"

"A ghost," I said.

"What do I need to do?" Dot asked.

Lu pointed at the side of the bed. "Why don't you sit here while Brogan and Stella get things sorted out."

"Your husband's here too?"

"Always," Lu said.

"You've done this a lot, haven't you?" Stella asked me.

"Enough to know how it works best for Lu. You need to be calm. Her mind and the realm of the living are filled with sounds and emotions and textures and smells and colors that will feel like a car crash now that you've passed."

She cringed. I instantly regretted my choice of words. "Bad example," I said. "My apologies. But it's going to feel overly…everything. Loud, vivid, smelly. Life is chaos."

"Okay," Stella said. "Stay calm and ignore her memories. Has life been bad for her?"

"Very."

Oh, there were good times too. Those memories might be just as strong as the bad times. But I knew Lu. She'd lock the good times, the times of us being together, the awkward early days, that damn rodeo, the bakery, tea, the love, away as deeply as she could.

That was all she had left of us. She wouldn't want to share it with anyone else.

"All right," she said. "It's going to be startling. Is there anything else I need to know?"

"Think about exactly what you want to say to your sister and say it first. If it's too hard for you, if it's too much for Lu to bear, I'm going to yank you out of there by the hair." I smiled to soften the words, but the threat was very, very real.

Stella held my gaze for a moment, then everything about her steadied. No more wide eyes, no more nerves. This was her shot, her best chance to say whatever she wanted to say to her sister that had kept her from moving on from this world.

"You won't have to do that," she said.

I believed her.

"Quick and focused," I said. "Stay out of her memories. Don't let the living world overwhelm you."

"Got it."

"Ready?"

She shook her hands and bounced on her toes a

little. I wondered if she had been a gymnast when she was younger.

"I'm ready," she said.

I stood next to the bed, my legs half in and half out of the little night table. The table was new, and I barely even noticed it. The only voice it carried was a very soft humming, maybe the worker who had assembled it, maybe just echoes from the old wall and floor it sat against.

"Lu," I said, placing my hand on her shoulder. "We're ready."

"Ready?" Lu asked Dot.

Dot nodded.

"Brogan's going to help Stella step into me. It's not…easy. So give us a few minutes to sort everything out."

"I will."

"Do you know what you want to say to her?"

Dot nodded. "That I love her. And miss her. And I'm so sorry for what I did."

"Okay, that's okay," Lu said. "Give me a minute." Lu turned her hand up on her knee, palm waiting for mine.

I held out my hand for Stella, who quickly took it in hers.

"I'm the connection," I said. "I am here to close the circuit between life and death and all the ways a soul can be caught between them. I'll hold this space so you can come back to it. So you're not lost to Lu's memories. So you don't burn to ash when you're exposed to the raging fire of life."

Stella licked her lips, a little startled at my description, but she nodded.

Tough, this one. Made of unbreakable determination.

I liked that about her.

I took two seconds, maybe three, finding my center. There was a cost for all of us in this. Lu carried the highest risk. Not only would she have to endure the physical pain, ghosts were not very stable entities.

It was easy for a ghost to lose focus in the chaos of being part of the living world again. If the host wasn't strong enough, if the will of the ghost wasn't strong enough, if the connection wavered, even a fraction, the entire thing could go to hell in seconds.

A spirit could be torn to shreds, a bloody, ragged mess of a thing that either blew apart into dust specks—deader than dead—or shattered and *stuck* inside the host.

Most living people wouldn't survive having fractured bits of the dead inside them, and the ones who did, eventually went mad.

I started humming the Little Bird song, urging the bird to fly through the window because there was molasses candy on the other side.

Stella raised her eyebrows as I went on to the chickadee verse. I ignored her. The song helped me focus. I'd used others in the past, but once I'd heard this one, it had stuck and was now my go-to ghost-hosting focus.

"All right. This is gonna be easy," I said. "Nothing but duck soup. One, two..." I reached down and finally pressed my hand into Lu's palm, my long, strong fingers wrapping around hers, "...three."

The hot jolt of energy flashed through me so hard, I shook like a tin house in a desert wind. It was—

—*black powder, lightning, fire*—

—it was—

—*storm through a forest, raging rivers carving earth, stone, mountains*—

—it was—

—*screech of joy, wail of loss, and voices, voices, voices, wanting, needing, loving, living, howling, begging, singing*—

—it was—

—*lu, Lu, LU*—

"There," I whispered, as the connection between worlds latched and held, *snick*ing together in the center of me, like a zipper from my head to my feet. "We're clear. You're clear, Stella." I wasn't looking at her, couldn't look at Dot. All I could see was Lu.

Lu, right there in her world, one set of zipper teeth sticking out into my world, Stella's world.

And where those two worlds met in me? Oh, the collision of color, heat, scents, *life*, that pummeled and shook me. I wanted to open my mouth and yell. I wanted to open my mouth and drink it down until it tore me apart. Blissful agony.

Instead I inhaled slowly, breath catching and smoothing. Then I widened my stance and set my shoulders, as if I were holding up the ceiling, the house, the world.

And exhaled.

"What do I do?" Stella sounded lost and small.

Wanting what was right there: an open doorway, a (mostly) living breathing body, a wonderful woman inviting her to step into her space, offering her a voice she hadn't had in years.

"Just walk through me and then to Lu. Don't stop. You'll fall into her. And when I tell you it's time to leave, you walk back through me. Got it?"

"Yes. I think so. Yes."

I was still watching Lu, and only Lu, but I felt Stella moments before she strode through me—

—anger, jealousy, hope, the horrifying collision, metal groaning, glass shattering, then, pain and blood, so much blood and the blackness before the light—

Stella passed through me, her stride steady, homed in on Lu like a heat-seeking missile.

Lu hissed and jerked, her head snapping back, exposing her long bare throat, her body bowed out away from the headboard. She swallowed and swallowed, a trickle of tears trailing from the corners of her eyes. Then she gritted her teeth and tipped her face forward again, the movement full of stops and starts, as if the person running her body wasn't used to the controls yet.

She sat straighter, smaller jerking motions as she pressed her back against the headboard again. Every line of her showed the pain she contained. The struggle.

She opened her eyes.

And that was not Lu.

I had forgotten. Forgotten how hard it was to see her like that, a passenger in her own body. Forgotten how angry it made me. How I wanted to rage and destroy and tear that invading spirit out of her with my bare hands.

"Steady," I said to myself, needing someone to say it, needing to hear it. We had all agreed to this. Agreed the price of Stella talking to Dot was worth the book she'd led us to. "Steady, man."

Lu opened her mouth, stopped, closed it again and cleared her throat. She nodded, one jerky little move, and tried again.

"Heya, Dotty."

Dot made a small sound, her hand flying to her mouth, fingers pressing her lips. Just as quickly, she pulled her hand away and settled, remembering that she had very little time.

"Stell? I'm so sorry. I didn't mean to make you mad. I never meant what I said. I was just angry about you dating Paul. I was such a selfish child."

"No, that's why I'm here," Stella said. Her intonation was wrong, slightly longer in the vowel than Lu. It was unsettling. "Stop blaming yourself. I wasn't all that mad when I drove off."

"You were," Dot insisted. "You were so angry at me."

"All right, yes. I was angry when I left. But I was halfway to Chicago and having a good time. A good drive. I was going to come home and tell you I was going to marry Paul, just to make you squirm at every family get-together."

"Oh," Dot said, nodding. "That would have been fine. Really, it would have been wonderful."

Stella smiled and leaned forward, a smoother

motion than all the others. "Oh, don't buckle after all these years. Paul was a jerk."

Dot choked on a laugh. "He really was. You deserved so much better than him."

"I know that now. I think I knew it then. But he wasn't on my mind when I…when I crashed the car. I wasn't mad. I wasn't angry at you."

"You should have been. I was horrible to you. I can't believe the last thing I said to you was in anger."

"You were worried. You had good reason to be. But you weren't the reason for my accident. Or for my death." She smiled, and I sucked air in through my teeth. She had a nice enough smile, loving and forgiving and a little sad, but it was not Lu.

I wanted to slap that look off her face. Wanted to pull her out of Lu and throw her into the next county.

Instead, I clenched my hands into fists, tight enough my knuckles cracked.

"If I could take it back, everything I said, all those awful things, I would," Dot said. "I love you. I miss you. I gave my daughter your name because I wanted her to carry a part of someone who is so special to me. My only sister."

"Poor girl," Stella said, "I've always hated my name."

Dot absently wiped the tears off her cheeks with the backs of her hands and laughed. "She doesn't like it either."

Stella chuckled. Then she held out her hands, Lu's arms raising, the wrists bent, fingers dangling like a marionette before Stella corrected and straightened her hands.

Dot scooted closer, crossing her legs so her knees touched Lu's, and grabbed her hands eagerly.

"I don't have a lot of time, but I need to tell you a few things. So just listen, okay?" Stella said.

Dot nodded.

"I love you. I love Mat and am so glad you married him. I love your kids. I've seen them as they grew up here, watched them move away. I love that you raised them here in our house, in our home. And I think renting the place out is perfect. Plus, whoever you put in this room I can spy on—so make sure you book all the hot guys in my room."

Dot snorted, it was a little wet and sniffly, but it was still a laugh. "Promise."

"I can't do ghost things, like move objects or make sounds, so if you were thinking you could use that in advertising, don't."

"I'd never do that to you."

"Unless I asked?"

"Of course. If you wanted, I'd take out front page ads in every paper in Illinois."

Stella tittered. It was high and delicate, and not Lu.

I inhaled. Exhaled. Started the countdown from one hundred.

"I'll be waiting for you. When you pass, I'll be right here for you. We'll step into that light together. And if anyone else passes before you, I'll be there for them. You let them know that, okay? That Stella is here, knitting, happy, and waiting to help them through the light."

"I'll tell them." Dot wasn't even trying to stop the tears now. They rolled in a constant stream, blotching her face with red, turning her nose pink.

"And I want you to know I had a book once. It was magic. Real magic. I hid it in the shed. I tried to give it to Lu and Brogan in exchange for this conversation. That man stole it from Lu. She's the rightful owner now. But I don't want you to get mixed up in all that. I do want you to know that magic is real. And dangerous. And sometimes wonderful.

"But you should stay away from it, okay?"

"Sure," Dot said. "I never even thought it was real, and I stayed away from it. It won't be hard to stay away from it now."

"We owe a big thank you to Lu and Brogan."

"Yes," she agreed.

"Maybe give her a few bucks off her bill?"

Dot huffed a laugh again. "Oh, she's staying for free. Anytime. As long as I own the house. And I'll book her in this room so you can talk to…Brogan."

"Unless there's a hot guy who wants to stay. Then you book the hot guy."

"Hot guy gets the room, then Lu, then everyone else. Promise."

Lu jerked, and her eyes fluttered shut before opening again.

"That's it," I said. "Time to leave, Stella."

"What? No," she said. "It can't be so soon. Just a minute. Just a little more, please."

Lu shuddered again, and Dot clenched her hands tighter steadying her through the tremor.

"What is it?" Dot asked. "Are you okay?"

"Stella," I warned.

"I love you, Dotty. I'm proud of you. I'm waiting for you. But don't come see me for a long, long time, okay? I want to see you become a great-great-great grandma at least."

"I'll do my best. I think Summer Stella might be thinking about kids in the next couple years."

"Oh, she's been doing more than thinking about them."

"Is she pregnant?" Dot asked, then she shook her head. "No. Don't tell me. If she wants me to know, when she wants me to know, she'll tell me. I love you, Stella. I wish we'd had forever together."

"We will," Stella said, as another hard tremor shook Lu. "Just not yet."

"Now, Stella," I said. "Or I'm reaching in there and pulling you out by your teeth."

"I need to go. But remember, I'll be right here. If you want to talk, or just want someone to listen, I'll be here."

Dot nodded and nodded, her voice too choked up for words. "I miss you, little sister. I love you," she squeezed out.

Lu was shaking and shaking, as if she were buried in a snow bank, freezing to death. "S-same here, big s-sister."

"Out," I demanded.

Stella turned Lu's face to me. I held my hand for her. If she'd take it, I could help pull her into this reality. If she didn't take it, I was going to shove my hand in there and yank.

Stella managed to lift Lu's hand. Even though I had dulled senses when it came to the living world, when Stella dropped Lu's hand into mine, even I could tell it was cold, cold, cold.

Too cold.

"Walk to me, right now, Stella. Right the hell now."

Lu's eyes closed, her teeth chattering, body trembling. Dot held on to her other hand, crying silently, watching, but not understanding. Not fully.

"Three," I said, "two, one."

Stella hesitated, and I knew in that moment she'd lost herself. That seeing her sister had broken her concentration. That she had seen some of Lu's memories, some of her life. Sorrow and then horror twisted her features. Her mouth dropped open in a hollow "O" as if she were hurting so much, she didn't have the air to scream.

If Stella didn't step forward, if she didn't disentangle from Lu and enter the ghostly realm again, those memories, Lu's brilliant, hard, horrifying life would tear her apart.

"Fuck it." I gripped Lu's hand tighter, and then allowed my hand to sink *into* hers.

Stella was there. Cold and slippery like frozen silk. And Lu was there too.

Everything about Lu was fire and warmth. She was home and peace and love, and I could hear her memories calling to me, our memories. I could feel her reaching for me.

Even though it would be disastrous for me to reach

back, any second longer leaving Stella there, possessing her body, making it more and more possible that she would never be able to be free of her, I paused.

"Brogan?" Lu's voice, Lu's heart so strong, her emotions a wave of water, heavy enough to drown me, an ocean of death I'd welcome. That one word, my name, carrying every emotion of a long, long life wanting, lonely, loving, angry, determined.

"Lula," I breathed. My voice echoed softly, as if being repeated by polished bells, hung waiting in the still air.

"I love you," she said, just as she always did.

"I love you."

And there was more, so much more to say, my senses drowning in the scent of flowers, in the warmth of her pulse, the thrum of her spirit, the echo of her soul in me reaching for home, just as my soul in her reached toward me.

It would be easy to stay here. To touch and remain, to hold, to lose myself in her and keep her for all the time I had left.

But Stella was there, cool and slick, spreading out too thin, like a membrane between Lu and me, a thin, wailing wall that was tattering with each beat of Lu's heart.

"Please," Lu said, her voice straining.

It broke me. "Yes," I agreed, even though I didn't know what she was asking. I would do anything. Anything for her.

"Stay," she breathed.

"Dotty?" Stella howled, a far-off cry that somehow

felt like it was surrounding me, swallowing me whole. It was that, the sister crying, lost, her thoughts spinning, as if caught by a hard wind, her form failing with each *thump, thump, thump*, that shook me free from taking that last step. From falling into Lu and never leaving.

I am a strong man. I had spent years holding on to hope, years being beside Lu and still alone. I'd walked every step of this path with her, every second, minute, hour—and days, days, endless days.

But it took everything I had to pull myself from the siren call of Lu's body, her soul, her heart and turn instead to Stella's failing presence.

Just my hand. It was just my hand joined with Lu's, but it also carried all of my attention, my focus, my will.

I flexed my fingers. Stella was thinner, her voice so distant, it was a mosquito buzz. But she was there, not shattered yet. Close, so close, but still whole.

I focused on her, all my will, all my intention, and gently gathered the thin, thinner, thinnest cloth of Stella into my palm. It was like trying to catch the frozen wind and fold it into a pocket square.

For a moment, I thought I'd waited too long. That I was too late and she would be lost, torn apart into tatters, shattered inside of Lu, but then I could feel the weight, feather-light in my palm, becoming heavier and heavier as I flexed my fingers and drew more of her toward me.

It felt like I was suspended there forever, pulling the ghost's soul and spirit to me, while Lu called to me. I wanted nothing more than to run straight into the fire of Lu.

And then…

….I pulled.

"Dotty?" Stella was sitting in the chair in the corner, just as I had first seen her, the knitting unspooled in her lap, needles tucked into the ball of ghostly yarn. She looked shocky, blurry at the edges, weak and thin, as if shadows had eaten up the bulk of her.

I was still standing in the middle of the little side table, but had swiveled my hips to throw Stella like I'd been hauling on a rope.

I twisted to face Lu again.

She had collapsed against the headboard. Her eyes were open and staring blankly at the edge of the wall where it met the ceiling.

Dot held her hand and was shifting to one side to give Lu room to stretch out. Encouraging her to wake up.

"It's okay," Dot said. "Everything's okay. You're okay. Just keep breathing. Can you hear me? Are you okay?"

I exhaled and took one more dangerous step closer to Lu. When I stretched out my hand, it trembled. I gently brushed her cheek.

"Come on, love. You need to come back for me."

A heartbeat, two, then life filled her blank eyes and she blinked.

"There, now, there." Dot patted Lu's hand and fussed with the coverlet, moving it so Lu's legs could unbend from the cross they were in. "Let me help you lie down. Just Lu, not Stella now, right? Lu?"

Lu groaned softly and dragged her hand up to her head like there was a bowling ball attached to it.

She squeezed her eyes closed, and another soft groan escaped her lips.

"Lu?" Dot asked.

"Yes," Lu barely breathed.

"Water? Aspirin?" Dot was on her feet. She'd dried her face and wiped her tear-streaked fingers on her pants. She was all business now, and I appreciated that she was putting Lu's needs in front of her own need to process the conversation with her sister. The forgiveness, the reminder of love.

"Yes," Lu barely whispered. She was moving like she was weighted down by boulders, working her legs out one at a time, inch by inch, as she slowly rolled onto her side, away from the window.

"I'll be right back. Stella, Brogan, keep an eye on her." Dot's cheeks were hot red, but she nodded to the chair where Stella was sitting, as if it were totally natural to talk to an empty space.

"We will," Stella said, happiness coloring her voice. She was starting to look a little more solid, and upon hearing her sister use her name, didn't seem quite so in shock. "Is Lu okay?"

"She will be." I tried not to blame her for Lu's condition, but obviously I wasn't all that successful.

"I'm sorry. I just couldn't find my way back. There were too many, so much...her life...oh, Brogan, how do either of you hold on? How are you both still alive?"

"Love," I said, not looking away from Lu. I bent and brushed my fingertips across her hair, wishing I could tuck it behind her ear as she curled up, her face, pressed into the soft pillow, paler than the white fabric.

She stretched one hand out across the remaining space of the bed, looking for me, reaching for me.

"I'm here. I got you." I opened and closed my hands a couple times, reminding myself that I couldn't get lost in her again. Not if we were both going to come out of this alive.

I lowered myself to the edge of the bed and stretched in the narrow space there, facing her, my arm up over the top edge of her pillow, my other arm across her waist, hand resting on her back.

She tipped her head down more, instinctively knowing where my chest was, needing to burrow in closer to me.

She was asleep before Dot returned with the water.

CHAPTER FIFTEEN

Lu only got up once in the middle of the night. She drank the glass of water and took the aspirin Dot had left by the bed, then groped her way to the bathroom, eyes shut, and ran hot water into the bath. It took her a couple tries to get out of her clothes. I hissed when I saw the bruises down her arms and legs.

Some of those bruises were huge and swollen, others were fingerprint size, as if ghostly fingers had been pressing from beneath her flesh, trying to scrabble a way out from under her skin.

I sat with her while she lingered, eyes still closed, lights off, in the water, bunching up so it covered her chest to her chin but left her knees poking out of the water like two islands in a sea.

"I'm okay," she whispered. "Just tired. I'm okay."

"Yeah, you are," I said, from where I had lowered myself onto the floor so that I was sitting next to her, but opposite, my feet toward her head, her feet toward mine. "Just rest. Just rest, love."

She waved one hand through the water, her palm tipping up for a second. I would have taken it, but she shifted, crossing her arms over her ribs. Her breathing evened out as she slept.

I watched to make sure she didn't slip down and drown, and after about a half hour, I was sure the water had cooled off, so I woke her gently, by calling her name and touching her cheek until she stirred.

She toweled off and, wrapping the towel around her, found her way back to the bed, tucking under the covers before falling asleep again.

"You are so going to regret not brushing your hair before you fell asleep," I told her.

She didn't stir.

I needed to check on Lorde, because I'd promised, and because I was worried about her, too, but I didn't want to leave Lu behind.

"I have to go check on Lorde, love," I said.

"I can watch after her," Stella said. I'd forgotten she was in the chair still. "If anything happens, I can come get you."

I didn't want anyone looking after her but me, and certainly not the person who had been a big part of why Lu was hurting, but I didn't have much of a choice. I nodded tightly. "I'll be at the vet's. In the back. I'll be back in a few minutes."

I moved, not waiting for her to reply, because I was still angry at her, even though that anger was unjust.

The world was a blur, empty to me, unreal, and then I stood in the vet's office in front of Lorde's kennel.

Leon was sleeping on the cot opposite the kennels, on his side facing them. Lorde was the only animal there tonight, and she lifted her head the moment I arrived.

"There you are, pretty girl." I crouched and pushed my hand through the bars so I could pet her head. "How are you feeling?"

She wagged her tail, and her mouth opened, showing that ridiculous black-tongue smile of hers.

"Lu's doing fine. I'm doing fine too. We'll be here in the morning to pick you up."

She made as if to move, but I scratched under her chin. "Stay," I said. "Stay here. We'll see you in a couple hours."

I shifted my hand again to scratch behind her ears, then stroked her back, careful of the bandaging wrapping her leg. She finally settled back down, laying her head on her front paw, her eyes trained on me, slowly, slowly closing.

When I finally stood and stretched the stiffness out of my back, she was snoring softly.

I checked on Leon, who hadn't stirred, then I returned to Lu's side.

"She's been asleep this whole time," Stella said, as she continued with her knitting. "Dot peeked in once and put more aspirin and water by the bed."

I grunted in acknowledgment. Even though I didn't sleep, I was exhausted. So I settled into bed next to Lu and closed my eyes, letting the soothing clacking of ghostly knitting needles tick away the time.

"R eally?" Lu grumbled. "You let me sleep on wet hair?" She tugged the brush, trying to get it through her tangled red curls. "You promised you'd never let me do this to myself."

I sat on the edge of the bathtub, watching my wife snarl at the mirror. She was beautiful. Still pale and moving slowly from the experience yesterday, but vibrant. Alive.

"Honey, I couldn't have woken you up if I'd tried. How about braiding it for the day?"

"Fine. I'll braid it. But I'm going to buy that fancy detangler that smells like cookies, and you're gonna have to deal with it making you hungry."

I chuckled. "Noted."

"The truck's done," she said, as she pulled her hair back with both hands. She split it into thirds and began the simple, soothing act of setting her unruly hair into one long rope that hung over her left shoulder.

"I know. Lorde's ready to be picked up too."

She nodded, not really looking at her reflection in the mirror. "I know I have to follow Hatcher."

"But?"

"But I'm going to talk to Jo. Make sure she doesn't want to rethink storming out of here over one little misunderstanding."

"Maybe she's not interested in Sunshine, babe. Maybe she's not interested in settling down."

Lu pulled a rubber band out of her front pocket. "I think she is. Looking for a place to settle down. And I don't know why, but…I think this might be a good place for her. Even if Calvin isn't the person she wants to be with."

"There's a god who deals with all of this stuff, you know, Lu. Love is complicated. Hell, life is complicated, ours more than most. Maybe we should just let this be. Hit the road, find that journal."

"I'm thinking you just want to get in the truck and go," she said. "But I'm going to pick up Lorde and talk to Jo first. Then we'll see what we'll see."

"Which is code for you can't resist one more chance to meddle." I sighed, even though I wasn't really upset about this.

How could I be upset that somehow, even after all these years, even after all this pain, the woman I loved was still trying to find love in the world, joy in the world? She had no reason to do so, not with how the fates had treated us, how the gods had ignored us. But she still saw good in the world.

I refused to take that away from her.

"You have toothpaste on the corner of your mouth." I stood and reached for her just as she pressed her thumb on the edge of her lip. I pressed my thumb over hers, and her eyes fluttered shut at my touch.

I didn't move. She didn't move.

Nothing in the world moved but the beating of her heart.

"I love you," she whispered.

"I love you," I replied, my voice rough with tears I couldn't shed. Not yet. Because I hadn't given up on us. Wouldn't give up on us.

"Let's go get the dog, the truck, and see if we can help these two kids fall in love. It's a freaking country song, Lu. Our life's a damn country song."

I don't know how much of that got through to her, but some of it must have. She laughed, just a little chuckle in her chest. And if there was a glitter of tears in the corners of her eyes, I pretended not to see.

Dot didn't want us to go.

"Are you sure?" She stood in front of the lobby door, holding the latch so Lu couldn't pass. "I'd be happy for you to stay here for a little longer. For as long as you want. I have that cushion for Lorde we can put in the room. You know I'd love the company while she's recovering. You know Stella would too."

Lu wore black jeans, combat boots, and a pale green tank top that made her braid look like a river of fire over her shoulder. "I thought Stella wanted you to book a hot guy."

Dot's eyes widened. She tittered and nodded. "She did. I'm going to too. Maybe advertise for a male stripper?"

"Whoa!" I laughed.

"If you don't, she'll never forgive you," Lu said, somehow with a straight face.

Dot smiled, but her eyes were starting to go wet. "I don't know how I can ever thank you. How I can…"

Lu pulled her into a sturdy hug. "You're welcome. That's all. That's enough."

Dot nodded and gave Lu an extra squeeze before stepping back. "Any time you come through here, any time at all, you are welcome in my home. In my sister's home too."

Stella floated into the room and stood next to Dot. "She's such a softy," she said. "If Lu doesn't leave now, she's going to have to draw a name for the family holiday gift exchange."

I grunted, and wisely didn't say anything about how Stella was looking a little choked up herself.

"Thank you," Lu said. "If I come through here again, I'll be sure to stop by."

"Do that. Please do that. You'll never have to pay for a room here. This is your home too. If you want it. When you need it."

"As long as there aren't hot guys staying here," Stella added. "Well, probably then too. Dot has a blow up mattress that fits in her office."

Dot finally stepped aside and opened the door.

"Good-bye, Stella," I said. "Don't steal any more magic books, okay?"

"Wait," she said. "I'm sorry you didn't get your part of the deal. I'm sorry that man took it."

I rubbed at my chin, scratching at the stubble there that never grew into a full beard. "It wasn't in your control. I know that."

She bit her lip, glanced at Dot, glanced at Lu, who had hefted her duffle to her shoulder again and was walking out the door.

"There's another magic item," Stella blurted.

"There are a lot of magic items," I said.

"Not like this one. I saw it. A half-staff carved with creatures and symbols and runes. The woman who rented out the room a few years ago had it with her. It glowed. And everything on the staff *moved*."

Magic was a lot more common than people suspected. It was in the soil, in the air, in all of our blood. Still, magic items, real magic items, were carefully guarded, protected, and most of all: hidden.

Lu made a lot of money off real magical artifacts. When she found them.

"You remember the woman's name?"

She closed her eyes, her lips moving like she was paging back through her memories. "Betsy...no, Betty. Yes, that's it." She opened her eyes. "Betty Moss."

"Betty Moss. All right. Thank you."

She nodded. "What you gave me, well, that's invaluable. If I see anything else that comes through here, I'll let you know when you come back."

"*If* we come back."

She smiled. "You will. Dot's probably going to bribe the sheriff to arrest you if you drive down the highway and you don't stop in first."

"Good to know." Lu was out the door now, walking, even though Dot had offered, repeatedly, to drive her to the vet's office.

It was time to say good-bye. Time to leave.

"Safe travels, Stella," I said, in the common way of those who drove the Route.

"Safe travels, Brogan. I hope you find the answers you're looking for. You deserve it. You both deserve some answers."

I was already striding through the door, but I waved my hand in acknowledgment. I hated that she had any of Lu's memories, that she had gotten to relive even a moment of our life together. Even if some of those moments were sorrow and horror.

I knew she meant well, but I was jealous to hold what we had to ourselves.

Lu walked a steady pace. I fell into place beside her.

"Hey, love," I said.

She tipped her hand up at her side, and I pressed my palm into hers.

"Love you too," she said.

CHAPTER SIXTEEN

L orde couldn't stop wagging her tail. Her ears were velvety peaks, her mouth open, black tongue lolling and happy. Lu knelt in front of her, her forehead against the side of Lorde's head, scratching behind her ears softly.

"You'll need to change the dressing twice a day for the first few days," Dr. Carter said. "You should be able to take off the wrap in a week, or when she starts using her leg without limping. She's going to heal nicely as long as she doesn't overdo it in the first few days. No running, no climbing stairs. Can you lift her into your vehicle?"

Lu nodded, still draped over Lorde, fingers buried in her fur.

The truck was still at Sunshine's garage. I'd tried to steer Lu there first this morning, but she'd been determined to get Lorde before anything else. Including food.

But she wasn't going to make Lorde limp around

town to pick up the truck or food. She'd called for a Lyft driver, who was waiting outside.

"Just give her pain medication and antibiotics according to the schedule here," Dr. Carter made a note on the prescription pad, "and check in with a vet a month from now, or if you see anything odd with the wound."

"We got it," I said. "Old hands at dealing with wounds. She's going to be fine, Lu."

Lu nodded again, and with a breath, finally let go of Lorde and stood. Lorde tipped her head my way and wagged her tail harder until I reached down and took over the scratching behind her ears.

"Thank you," Lu said, accepting the piece of paper and the little bag with the bottles of medicine. "I really appreciate you taking such good care of her."

"She was a brave girl. I'm happy she's on the mend. But no more bullets, Lorde, okay?"

Lorde just sat there enjoying my fingers stroking behind her ears.

"Leon," I pushed to Lu. "He stayed with her last night. Did a good job."

"Tell Leon thank you for staying the night with her too."

The doctor smiled, obviously surprised that Lu would have remembered the man who took the night shift for Lorde.

"I'll tell him. He said she slept straight through."

"Good. Thank you again," Lu said.

"We're happy to have been here," Dr. Carter said. "I

certainly hope things settle down. No more excitement in the future, okay?"

Lu gave her a small smile and a wave, because saying she would never be on the wrong side of a gun when a magical item was involved would be a promise she couldn't keep.

Lorde stood and limped to Lu's side, her injured foot touching the ground for half a second before she put her weight on the next foot.

Lu opened the door for her. I passed through the wall to meet them on the other side.

"Good girl, Lorde," I said.

The Lyft driver, Tom, was a kid with a Black Hawks hat on backward and a collection of chin zits. He looked like he'd just escaped middle school, but he produced ID that said he was twenty-one. He pushed off the hood of the Dodge Durango I figured he had borrowed from his parents, just as Lu crouched down.

"Want me to help you with her?"

"I got her," Lu said, straightening with a hundred pounds of dog in her arms. "Get the door?"

"Yeah, sure. Hold on." He snapped to it, opening the back door, then jogging around to the other side and opening that door so he could reach half way through to help get Lorde settled.

Lorde eased out of Lu's arms and found a comfortable place on the seat facing the side window so she could rest her head on the edge of the door.

"You want to sit up front?"

"No, I'll ride back here with her."

"Yeah, good. Okay." He buckled the seatbelt,

checked his mirrors, and put the car in drive. "Where to?"l

"Fisher's Automotive."

"Is Calvin working on something for you?"

"My truck."

"Good choice. He's like the truck whisperer. I've got a 1960 Dodge D100 short bed he's helping me restore. He's got a knack for bringing old things back to life."

"Sounds like he knows him pretty well," I said from the front seat. I spread out, enjoying the leg room.

"How well do you know him?" Lu asked, picking up on my comment.

"Calvin? He's my cousin. Good guy. He had a chance to take over ownership of this big shop in St. Louis, but he turned it down. Said this was the family business. He wanted to stay here in McLean to take care of family. He thinks almost everyone in town is family."

"Don't even start with me," I warned Lu. "Sunshine had his chance with Jo, and he blew it. He might be a nice guy, but maybe he's not the right nice guy for her."

Lu petted Lorde and stared out the window. She was thinking awfully hard about something, but I wasn't sure what.

"I love you," I said.

How I loved to see that little secret smile.

~

I hadn't expected the fight.

"Whoa," Tom slowed the car in front of the garage. "That's, uh… I'm sure it's not what it looks like."

"Looks like Jo's about ready to punch your cousin in the schnoz," I said.

Sunshine stood in front of the open bay doors, his arms crossed over his chest, both thumbs sticking out from under his armpits. His mouth was set in a hard line, his nostrils flared. He looked like a mountain facing a storm.

And what a storm she was. Jo's hands were loose at her side. But everything else about her was spoiling for a fight, from the angle of her shoulders, to her stance, to the tension in her spine.

"If you want to come back later," Tom said, "I could take you somewhere to wait for this to blow over. Want breakfast? A cup of coffee?"

"No," Lu said. "Just drop me off here." She had that determined look in her eye as she turned away from the scene of a fight that was about to explode and gathered Lorde into her arms. "Get the door for me, Tom."

"Yeah," he said. "Sure thing. Hang on."

He put the car in park and was around to the door in a flash.

"Let it go, Lu," I said. "It's just not gonna work out. They're oil and flame. Explosive. We need to get the truck, pick up some food, and hit the road."

Lorde grunted softly as Tom helped Lu exit the car. I

sighed and climbed out too, planting my hands on my hips and taking in the scene.

"Morning," Lu said.

"Lu." Sunshine's voice was as tight as a fist down a pipe. He glanced over at her and immediately uncrossed his arms. "What happened to Lorde? Holy shit, let me help you with her, hang on." He jumped into action and had his hands in place to take Lorde away from Lu, but Lu shook her head.

"Is the truck done?"

"Yes, it was ready last night. I left you a message. I wondered— What happened to her?"

"She was shot."

You would have thought Lu had brought the gun with her and was waving it around.

The three men working in the garage all strode out, wiping hands on rags, a sort of protective swagger shared between them, as if they were brothers more than co-workers.

"When?" Jo was all motion, too, moving along with Lu who was carrying a very alert tail-wagging Lorde toward the main door to the building.

"Yesterday."

"Out by Dot's place?" Sunshine asked. "I heard there'd been gunshots, but didn't know anyone had been hurt. Poor girl. Who would shoot a pretty girl like you?"

"An asshole," Jo said. She'd made it to the door before any of us and opened it. She stepped inside the little lobby, looking for a place for Lu to set down Lorde.

"I hope you called the cops on whoever did this,"

Sunshine said. "But if you didn't, just give me a description, and I'll do a little civil disobedience."

"Okay," I said, "maybe he has his good points."

"Where can I set her down?" Lu asked.

Jo glanced at Sunshine, then they both said, "the office," at the same time. Calvin headed out into the work bay while Jo ushered Lu down the hall to the office. She open the door and Calvin reappeared with a couple heavy moving blankets and spread them on the floor in the corner.

Lu knelt. Lorde stepped out of her arms and stood there for a moment, her head tipped up, that black tongue out as she panted, tail wagging, happy to be there.

"Ray," Sunshine asked one of the guys lingering in the doorway. "Get us some water for her?"

"You got it, boss." He left, and the other two men crowded up the doorframe, but didn't step into the small space.

"You need anything else?" the taller of the two asked.

"No, we're good," Sunshine said.

"You didn't even ask Lu," Jo said.

He glared at her. She glared back.

"Here we go," I said, settling in near the old file cabinet. "A match made in heaven. Don't they look like they can't wait to write love sonnets?"

Lu threw a look my way.

I chuckled. "Okay, okay. I'm just saying that truck is never gonna be called Silver."

"Coffee would be nice," Lu said.

"Decent name, but doesn't really do it for me," I said.

Jo and Sunshine broke off the staring contest and turned to her. It didn't take a genius to see that Lu was exhausted and pale. Jo caught on first.

"How do you like it?" Jo asked. "They have one of those nice, single-serve machines in the break room."

"You think it's nice?" Sunshine asked. He quickly shut his mouth, as if surprised he'd even spoken.

"It's, well, it's the kind that doesn't use those little pots that can't be recycled."

"I think those pots are the dumbest things," he said. "Why not use a pot that can be used for fresh grounds every time? We don't need to add more waste to the dumps."

Jo nodded. "What do you do with the grounds?"

"Give them to folks who like to put them on their gardens. Take some home for the flower beds."

"That's— Oh." Jo's face flashed pink, and her gaze skittered away, landing somewhere on the wall behind me.

"He's not that charming," I said.

"I like mine black?" Sunshine said.

That snapped her back into gear. "Who said I'm bringing you coffee?"

"No one. But I can hope?" The smile he gave her was bright as sunshine. Sunshine that pushed the clouds away and spun across the blue sky like the first fresh breath of spring promising long, warm summer nights.

Jo bit the side of her lip and narrowed her eyes, considering.

"Or not," he said, that smile still not wavering. "But Lu likes it with sugar, no cream."

Jo raised an eyebrow at Lu.

"And hot," Lu said. "Biggest cup you have."

"I'll be right back." With a quick look at Lorde, who had decided she'd done enough standing and was lying down now, Jo left the office.

"What are you doing?" Lu rounded on Sunshine, her finger jabbing the air between them.

"Uh… Getting you some coffee?" He glanced out the door Jo had just exited. "Why? Do you want something else?"

"I want to know why you and Jo are fighting."

He scowled, all the sunshine disappearing behind the shadow of frown lines.

"She has some kind of idea of me in her head, and I'm tired of trying to prove that idea isn't right."

"So you're yelling at her?"

"Who said I was yelling at her?"

"I did. I could hear you on the way over here."

"She can do that," I said. "Her hearing is amazingly sharp."

"So?" he asked.

"So that is not the way to tell someone you like them."

"Who says I like her?" His volume rose, loud enough that Ray, who had just returned with the water looked a little startled. Then a sly smile crossed his bearded face.

"Sure, boss," Ray said. "You like her. We can all see it."

"You… I don't." Sunshine rubbed a hand over the back of his neck. "Just put the water down before I fire you."

"Then who's gonna rebuild your carburetors?" Ray asked as he put the water beside Lorde and gently patted her head. "Good girl. Don't listen to Calvin. He's so in love he's snarling at everything that moves."

"You're fired," Sunshine said, with no heat.

"Yeah, yeah. I'm gonna get back to work, unless you want to deal with Mrs. Dutton today?"

Sunshine glared at him while Ray paused there at the door, hand on the latch.

"Tell Mrs. Dutton I said hello," Sunshine said.

"That's what I thought. Morning," he said to Lu. "Oh, and boss?" Ray said, turning the latch.

"What?"

"I think Jo's pretty great. You would be smart to tell her you haven't stopped talking about her since the moment she stepped into the shop."

"I don't pay you for your advice," Sunshine said.

"You should. Because I'm right. Aren't I? The very idea that Jo is leaving without you having a chance to explain things to her and see her again is killing you."

"Go away. We're no longer related."

"Just say, I'm gonna miss the hell outta that Jo when she's gone."

Lu crossed her arms over her chest and waited. Ray waited, the door almost free of the frame.

"You are the worst brother-in-law ever."

"Spit it out, brother."

"I'm gonna miss her like hell," Sunshine said, every

inch of him miserable. "Even though we just met, and I've made a fool out of myself. I just… I wish it had all been different."

Ray jerked open the door.

Jo stood there, two cups of coffee in her hands. She stared at Sunshine. He stared at her.

I groaned. "No. No way. One confession doesn't fix the fact that you two were about to go WWE outside just ten minutes ago."

"Hey, so, I got coffee." Jo walked over to Lu and handed her a huge mug in the shape of a stack of tires with "Starter Fluid" written across it.

"Thanks." Lu sounded smug. Way too smug.

"Oh, this isn't over yet," I said. "Just because she overheard a forced admission doesn't mean she's going to stay."

Jo handed Calvin his coffee next. He took it from her, and for a moment, they were both holding the mug.

"So are you two going to talk this out?" Lu asked. She pulled out the chair in front of the desk and lowered herself carefully into it. Hosting Stella had been hard on her, even though Lu had a much stronger constitution than a human. "Because I have the biggest cup of coffee in this room and more time to waste than the both of you put together."

"Your truck's done," Sunshine offered to throw her off the trail.

"That won't work," I said.

"Lorde and I could both use a few minutes of down-time before we hit the road. And since I'm the reason you two started off on the wrong foot— Don't give me that look. You were distracted the day you first opened the door and found her here. Saying things that you probably wouldn't have said. I was there. So," Lu pointed at Jo, then at the chair on the other side of the desk, "how about you both say what needs to be said."

I saw the exact second they both realized they could not outwait Lula Gauge.

Sunshine stepped away from the desk and leaned his hip against the window sill.

Jo dragged the chair out and away so she could see both Sunshine and Lu at the same time.

"You should know I am not in your corner, Sunshine," I said. "But if you're gonna have any kind of a shot with a person like Jo, you're going to have to talk honest."

"If I'd met you anywhere in the world," Sunshine said, "I'd say to myself: that's the most beautiful person I've ever seen. I'd find some way to try to catch your attention. I'd hope against all God-given sense that you'd see me. That you'd talk to me. Even once."

Jo blinked. She clasped her hands in her lap and nodded once.

Sunshine tipped his head to the ceiling, took a breath, then talked honest.

"I think you're out of my reach. You've lived in big cities. You've made your own path in the world, and you don't take shit from anyone. There's no reason you'd want to date me. I'm working in the town where I was born, in the business my father and grandfather ran. My employees are family, or friends who might as well be.

"And I don't ever plan on leaving McLean. My family's here. My roots are here. Besides all that, I like it. I like knowing every face in town—for good or bad. I like the pace, the quiet. I just…like my life. But now that I've met you, I'll always know it won't be complete."

"Calvin…" Jo said.

"Hold on. Just give me one more second, and I'll have said it all, okay?"

She nodded.

Lu drank coffee and threw me an intolerably smug look.

"One pretty speech isn't going to fix anything," I said.

"I know this was just a pit stop. Just one more job. But I want you to know, I'm going to remember you forever, Jo. Even if I never see you again."

"Bingo," Lu whispered so quietly, only I heard her.

"Not bingo," I said. "Jo has her own mind to make up. Don't you, Jo? Are you going to let this guy guilt you into something you might regret for the rest of your life?"

Lu scowled at me, and I gave her a wink. "All's fair in love and truck names."

"Let me get this straight," Jo said. "You think I've got it all together, working a road job for a crappy computer repair company, and you think you're falling behind being a business owner who is obviously a cornerstone of your town?"

"No, you're not seeing what I was…"

"Hush," Lu said. "Let her have her say. She listened to you."

He nodded and nodded, and wisely kept his mouth shut.

"I think we've both been assuming some things." Jo ran her fingers back across the shaved side of her head, then tugged on the earring at the top of her ear before clasping her hands together and resting her elbows on her knees so she could lean forward.

"Give me three questions."

He nodded.

"Answer them honestly."

Nod.

"One: Do you only like me because of the tats and piercings? Because I'm some *thing* you've never seen before?"

Oh, the anger behind those words. I didn't know all of the things that had happened in her past, but being an object to be scorned instead of a human being to be respected had to be one of them.

"No," he said. "I like those things, but that's not *all* you are."

"You better not be bullshitting me, Fisher."

"I'm not."

There was no doubting the honesty in his words.

"Well, I'll be damned." I moved over to where Lu sat and looked between the two people. "I gotta admit this isn't going how I expected."

Lu just waggled her eyebrows.

"Two." Jo held up two fingers. "Do you have any idea how these people you call *family* hate me?"

He lifted his head, asking for permission to speak.

"That wasn't a rhetorical question, Fisher. I expect

you to answer it."

"The people I call family don't hate you. They like you a lot. Ray sure is on your side more than mine."

"What about Doug and Keith?"

"Doug is an ass, and isn't welcome in my shop any longer. His views are not mine, and not the view of most people in this town. As for my brother." Calvin rolled his eyes. "I stopped taking his sorry-ass opinion as gospel when I was eight. He's a thick-headed jerk, who hasn't had to make room for anything in his life except his own ego."

"I heard you talking to him."

"I recall."

"You shared his opinion about me."

"Nope. No, I did not. I'm sorry if it sounded like I did, and I'd be happy in the future to clarify any and everything I say to him for you. But no. My brother and I do not see eye-to-eye on anything but making sure our mother doesn't kill herself remodeling that old house of hers."

"Okay," she said. "Okay." She sat back, but seemed even more tense.

"Last question."

He opened his mouth, then closed it and nodded. He looked like he was bracing for a hit or getting ready to catch someone falling off a cliff.

"Did you really mean what you said? About seeing me and…." She swallowed.

Sunshine opened his mouth.

Lu lifted one finger in warning, just as I said, "Stow it, Sailor."

He shut his mouth. Waited.

"What you said," Jo continued, "that you saw me? That you'd remember me?"

He waited a moment, then an extra beat after that. Jo waited too.

"Come on you two. You can do this," I said. "Take the chance. Leap for it. If it's love, you'll never regret a single, stupid minute of it. I promise. I promise."

Lu tipped her face up, her eyes closed, and turned her hand for me.

I took it in mine, because I always would. Always.

Sunshine walked toward Jo, then he knelt in front of her. He rested his fingers—just his fingers—on one arm of the chair. Not caging her in. Giving her room, giving her space.

"Every word I said is true. I… I don't know how to make you believe me, but from the moment I saw you… It's you, Jo. You're all I can see. All I…hope for. A chance. Just a chance to see if we can be… If there's something here. Between us. Together."

"And if it doesn't work?" she asked.

"We'll still be friends." He winced. "Well, after we get done being mad. I think we could be friends."

"What makes you think that?"

"Look at what we've gone through already. Diners with jackasses, brothers who are dumbasses, bossy customers."

"Hey," Lu said on a laugh. "Don't drag me into this."

I rolled my eyes hard enough it hurt. "Drag you into

this. Like anyone could drag you out of it. I know. I tried."

"It's been a lot in just two days," Jo said. "What if it's all boring from here on out?"

"Have you seen this town?" he asked. "Boring can be kind of nice."

Jo pressed her lips together, then ran her fingers over her hair again. "Okay. Like a date. Or two. Just to…try."

Sunshine smiled so hard I thought his face was gonna break.

"That's good. That's really great. That's good. So good."

I sighed and turned to face Lu. "Go ahead. Say it."

Lu grinned at me like she'd just eaten the last Twinkie in the apocalypse. "Calvin, did you say Silver's ready for me now?"

"Silver?" he asked, looking away from Jo with some effort and slowly rising.

"That's the name of my truck. I just named it. Silver. It's the perfect name, isn't it?"

I shook my head at the heavens and the gods who paid absolutely zero attention to losers like me.

CHAPTER SEVENTEEN

Lu ran her fingers over the steering wheel and adjusted the mirror that didn't need adjusting. She was always like this at the start of hitting Route 66 again. A little nervous, a little hopeful, a little resigned.

The road was two thousand four hundred forty-eight miles of twisting, lonely broken pavement. It had been our life for so many years now, there was a sort of desperate fear that we'd never know anything else. That we'd never see a different horizon.

"You don't have to follow it," I told her, like I did every time we returned to the Route we couldn't seem to escape. "You could book a flight. Hawaii. Scotland. Go see the world. I'll be here. I'll wait for you. Forever."

She turned her head, finding where I sat, slouched against the door, Lorde snugged up against my insubstantial leg. Lu's duffel sat at my feet. Even if I hadn't been Undead, there would have been plenty of room for her duffle, my feet, and at least another bag of gear in the spacious cab.

"You and me, Brogan Gauge. We are going to see this through to the end together. *Together*. Do you hear me?"

The fierceness of her, the fire that even all these long, sad years couldn't put out, burned hot and clean and dangerous.

"Yes, Ma'am, Mrs. Gauge. I hear you. Together. Always."

She rolled her shoulders, inhaled, exhaled, then started the truck.

It growled to life like a dream come true.

"There you go, Silver," Lu said. "Listen to that heart of yours. You're hungry for the road, aren't you?"

The truck, not being alive, didn't answer. But Lorde yawned and thumped her tail.

Lu put the truck in gear, then pulled out of the little stretch of pavement on the side of Fisher's Auto. She flipped the turn signal, then eased out into the sunny day.

"I'm thinking food soon," she said. "Maybe resupply in Lincoln or Springfield? I'm not stopping at a hotel tonight, so I'll need a sleeping bag."

"You can stop at a hotel. I can handle a hotel, Lu."

"We both need some rest. Away from people. Living people. Or ghosts with agendas. What about the Union Miners Cemetery in Mt. Olive? I'll get some sleep. You can see if any of Mother Jones's boys are up to shoot the shit."

"Works for me, love, though I still think you should get a room with a bed. You're exhausted."

She yawned, then cranked down the window just a crack to let a fresh breeze into the cab.

"I'll buy a mattress," she said. "And a pillow. I'd rather be in the graveyard with you than cooped up with all those beating hearts around me."

Right. There were reasons Lu didn't like hotels too.

"Why do I argue with her?" I asked Lorde. "She always wins." Lorde just huffed in agreement.

"You know I always win," Lu said with a quick glance over at Lorde. She stroked Lorde's soft black fur. "Sweet girl. You should not have done that. We are going to work on our *stay* commands. No more running in front of hunters with guns. Jesus, you know what could have happened?" Her voice broke there at the end, and tears gathered in the corners of her eyes.

That was my Lu. Cold as winter steel when shit was going down, and only allowing herself time to fall apart when the world rocked back to an even keel.

She rubbed at the corners of her eyes with the back of her forearm and blew a fast breath out between her lips. "I'm fine. We're good. We're all good."

"Ah, love." I stretched my arm up over the back of the bench seat, my hand resting gently in her hair. "How about a little music?" I suggested. "Something easy? Think the radio works?"

"I bet you want music," she said. "All right, rock or country? Or blues? What's your poison?"

"I'll bet you fifty bucks that radio won't get anything but random ham radio static."

"Let's find out." She turned the knob on the AM radio mounted flush under the ash tray in the center of the dash.

A crackly station came through the speakers, then "Cupid" by Sam Cooke crooned out, his soothing tenor clear as a bell as he asked Cupid to shoot an arrow to pierce a lover's heart.

Lu drove as the song played through, and when it was over, the DJ came on the air.

"That song is dedicated to Lu and Brogan, and all the lovers out there on the Route."

Lu scowled at the radio, then at me.

"Dot, maybe?" I said. No one else knew both of our names. Well, not in McLean.

Lu scanned the cracked, rough section of the two-lane road. We were coming up on Kickapoo Creek, I-55 buzzing with traffic to our left, the railroad tracks appearing and disappearing behind a wall of scrub trees to our right.

Nothing seemed amiss.

"This is DJ Bo, and you're listening to KUPD radio, all the love, all the songs. Listeners Lula and Brogan went out of their way to help a pair of young lovers fall in love. Isn't that nice? Broken hearts and people falling in love is what we're all about here at KUPD. So to celebrate Lu and Brogan's kind deed, we're giving them a prize!

"I'm out here on the other side of the Kickapoo Creek at the pullout on old Route 66. That's just north of Lawndale. Lu and Brogan, come on over and claim your prize."

There was something about that voice. Something that dug in bone deep.

Power.

Lu hit the brakes so hard, Lorde had to scrabble to keep from tumbling to the floorboards. Dust billowed up behind us rolling in a cloud over the truck, depositing a fine layer of grit on the window.

She snapped off the radio.

"What in the hell?" she whispered, her hand straying to the watch around her neck. Goosebumps prickled down her arm and red slapped over her cheeks and neck.

"That was a god. Brogan, that was a god."

"Yes, it was." I soothed Lorde who fumbled and turned so she could put her head on Lu's leg.

"Pretty sure it was Cupid," I said. "Let me go look. You just stay here a minute."

"Don't go anywhere." Lu's voice was rough. She was afraid I'd do something stupid. Well, afraid I'd do something stupid without her.

"We go together," she said. "We do this together. Don't you dare ghost out of here and face that god alone."

"We could turn around," I said. "Drive north."

"Cupid's the god of connections and destruction," she said. "He won't have any problem following us. Finding us. I don't want to live my life running from a god."

"We could bunker up somewhere with spells, hit the storage. Hope this—whatever this is—blows over." I had a good idea what this was. Lu had meddled in Cupid's business. And now the piper was demanding his pay.

"We haven't done anything wrong," she said.

I grunted.

"Nothing wrong to him," she said. "Jo and Calvin dating would have happened if we were there or not."

I made a fifty-fifty waggle with my hand. "We did an awful lot of interfering. I'm thinking we might just rename this truck the I Told You So, now that Cupid's on our ass."

I focused on those last words, filled them with my love and my laughter. Whatever mess we were in with the god, we'd handle it. No matter what the outcome, we'd handle it together.

"No," she breathed, pulling back her shoulders and straightening her spine. "We do this together. Face the god together, right, Brogan?"

"It'd be smarter to let me go see exactly what we're driving into."

"Don't you dare leave me," she said, her emotions still too close to the surface. Losing the book to a hunter had been hard. Stella possessing her had been harder. Lorde getting injured—shot to save Lula—had been the hardest.

She was tired, injured, holding on by a string. And now she had to face a god.

But not alone. Never alone.

I held my hand out for her, palm up. "Never alone, love. Not even when you're being stubborn and a little stupid because you're afraid. We are not helpless, you and I. And there hasn't been anything in this world that's been able to kill us yet."

She put her hand, palm down, over where mine was resting on top of Lorde's head. I squeezed it hard enough I imagined she might be able to feel my flesh, even though I knew she couldn't.

But she could feel my intention, my faith in us. Right now, that was all I had to give her.

"Let's drive, Lula. Let's see what the god wants."

Lu took her foot off the brake and headed toward the bridge.

It never ceased to surprise me how the freeway, running parallel to the Route, could be full of cars while the Route—a little shabbier, a little narrower, a little slower, a thing of the past—was largely ignored.

Right now I was grateful for it. There were no cars behind us and none ahead. Whatever was happening, wouldn't put innocent people in danger.

The bridge over Kickapoo Creek wasn't anything special. Built in 1954, the concrete parapet, with its squared off rails, stretched out ahead, the spaces between the rails and balusters sectioning sunlight and shadow out across the length of the bridge.

There was a man sitting on a beast of a motorcycle in the pullout—just a dirt, grass, and gravel shoulder to the left of the bridge where fishermen parked their vehicles while they rambled down to the creek in search of small mouth bass and channel catfish. The man glowed with power that moved and pulsed around him like refracted starlight.

Not a man, a god.

"He's on the other side," Lu said.

"Yeah, I see him." I could feel him too. The burn of his power stabbed the back of my neck, spread forward over my head like a giant hand had just grabbed me from behind and wrapped fingers over my chin and cheekbones.

"No deals," Lu said.

"No deals."

"No lies," Lu said.

"No lies."

"No fear," Lu said.

"No fucking fear. Go ahead, Lu. Get close."

She pulled across the bridge and turned into the pullout next to the god.

Cupid wore black denim, leather chaps, and a black jacket over a gray shirt that looked surprisingly soft and worn in. He was a big man—not as big as I am, but by no means small—bald headed with a long gray goatee topped by a mustache that could go for handlebar style if he wanted. He wore black leather and boots.

A diamond flashed at the top of his right ear and two gold hoops glinted in his earlobes. Colorful tattoos covered the side of his neck above his collar, disappeared underneath, and spread out across his hands, covering one with an angry owl and the word LEAD, the other with a dove and the word GOLD.

"Don't leave the truck," I said. I pushed through the passenger door and stood in front of Cupid, arms crossed over my chest.

"We don't meddle in the business of gods," I said. "We'd prefer you don't meddle in ours."

Cupid looked me up and down, from my boots to my eyes, and nodded once. "Brogan Gauge." His voice was the grumbling baritone of bars and neon and engines on the open road.

I heard Lu's quiet curse right before the truck door creaked open and her boots hit the gravel.

"I've heard of you and Lula," the god went on. "Of the attack. Of you two exchanging bits of your souls on the seam of Death's doorway. I'd wondered when our paths would cross."

"We don't want any trouble," Lu said. "And we don't have anything you'd want."

He leaned sideways, as if looking right through me was a problem. "Afternoon, Lula Gauge. Or should I say Lula Doyle?"

She pulled her chin up. "It's Gauge."

"Well, it would be if you had had a chance to take your wedding vows," the god said. "But you never had that chance, did you?"

This was not the god to challenge when it came to how things connected and joined.

Lu raised her eyebrows. "We took our vows. It doesn't matter if we never did it in front of a priest or judge."

"I happen to agree with you," he said. "Although the old-fashioned romantic in me likes the ceremony of marriage. Such a beautiful vow of love, of fealty. A memory never to be forgotten."

"Come on, Lu," I said, "Let's hit the road. Sorry to take up your time, Cupid. It is Cupid, isn't it?"

"I prefer to use the name Bo with people I know."

"You don't know us," I said just as Lu said, "I don't know you."

Cupid looked at me, leaned to look at Lu, and frowned. "This is awkward, isn't it? Here."

He snapped the fingers of his hand with GOLD written across the knuckles.

"What was that?" I asked.

"Brogan?" Lu asked, startled.

"I'm here, love," I said, not looking her way, still standing between her and the god. "How about you just go on your way, *Bo*?" I said. "No hit, no foul."

"I can't." He stood up off the motorcycle and stuffed his hands into the pockets of his jacket. "Well, not yet. I need to talk to you. To both of you."

"We're done talking," I said.

"Brogan." Lu's voice was so slight, I almost didn't hear her over the distant sound of the cars and trucks on the freeway. That softness, that worry, made me turn toward her. She reached out, her hand sliding into mine.

I clasped her palm tightly, as I always did, and felt flesh, warm, textured with ridges and lines, bones strong beneath skin softer than silk.

"Lu?" The world rocked under my feet, as I both tried to square myself steady to it and throw myself off it to reach for her.

She flew into my arms, body tight against mine, warm, real. I pulled her tight, tighter, the scent of her perfume mixing with the dust and oil of the road, the fast flutter of her pulse against my lips as I kissed the edge of her neck driving me senseless, wild.

"You're here, you're here, you're here," she whispered over and over as she clenched my shirt so hard she scratched the skin beneath. Welts were rising from her touch, but I didn't care.

I was solid, breathing. I could taste the sweat of her skin on my tongue, could feel the curves of her body, the hot wind curling between us like the sun itself was surprised to see us there, together.

My head hurt and my knees were threatening to buckle, but I didn't care. I was more alive than I'd been in years. Decades.

"I love you, Lu," I said. Just as I always said.

"I love you, Brogan," she replied. Just as she always did.

"Brogan, Lula," the god said, almost as if he regretted the interruption.

We turned toward him, but did not let go of each other. It wasn't the best defensive position to take in front of a god who could snap a person into and out of existence, but we'd been too many heartbeats apart.

A soft jingle of metal reminded me there was one more person on the road with us: Lorde.

"Stay, Lorde, stay," I said, but she limped over to Lu and I and wagged her tail at us, black tongue sticking out as if nothing was unusual about being in the presence of a god.

As if we weren't in danger.

Interesting.

"Well, who's this?" the god asked. "What's your name, pretty?" He crouched down and held his fingers out toward Lorde and wiggled them at her.

Lorde tipped her head one way, then the other, then limped over to him.

"Lorde," Lu said quietly, though whether a warning to the dog or answering the god's question, I didn't know.

"Just call me Bo." He produced a piece of bacon out of thin air, and Lorde immediately sat in anticipation of the treat.

"No. Lorde is my shepherd," Lu finished, dazed.

Bo snickered. "Even without the joke, that's a good name. Aren't you a sweetheart? Here you go girl." He offered the bacon. She took it daintily out of his hand and dropped it on the ground before eating it in small bites.

"Healing isn't my main power," he said, still crouched down and petting the softest part of Lorde's head right between her ears. "But if you'd let me, I could mend her leg."

Lu shook her head, but she clenched my shirt tighter, nails digging into my side. She was shaking, wound up so tight, I was afraid she'd fly to bits.

This was all too much. Too confusing to be facing a god who was offering us these moments and what appeared to be kindness to our dog.

We both knew it had to come at a cost too high for us to pay.

"No." I shifted my hold on Lu, wrapping an arm across her back and standing side-by-side with her against the god.

Together. Always.

The god stopped petting Lorde and stood, those

endless eyes weighing our worth. "You want to know why. Why I'm stepping in. Why now. What I'm offering. What you'll owe."

"That'd be a good start," I said.

He leaned back on his bike. It settled under his weight. Lorde watched him intently, wagging her tail. Then she sat, waiting for more bacon.

He slipped her another piece.

"I knew of you, both of you," he said. "How could I not? The way your souls are broken and mended, your lives connected and destroyed. Those are things I know."

"You were there when that monster jumped us?" I asked.

"No. Nowhere near you. I was in a little town near the ocean. Stepped away from the world for some time. But when I returned, I knew something terrible had happened to you. Just as many terrible things had happened to many, many people. Connection and destruction are powerful states of being, powerful events. It leaves a mark. And I feel them all."

"Rule them all," Lu said. "You rule them all. Make those connections and destructions happen."

Cupid tipped his head just a bit, considering her words. He nodded. "I make, allow, endure bindings and breakings. True. But I did not send your attackers. I was not a part of that event, that mark. Allowing this bond you carry, a soul for a soul," he pointed a blunt, inked finger between us, "I was a part of that. Made, and allowed to endure. If not for my grace, neither of you would be alive."

Lu tensed even more.

"If not for my grace," Bo went on, "you wouldn't have found that watch that gives you relief, moments when you can hear, see, feel each other."

"A woman named Rose gave us the watch," Lu said.

He smiled fondly. "Yes, she did. Insisted on it, until I agreed."

"Why?" I asked. "Why were we attacked?"

"I've asked myself that question for many years. And today... Well, today I have the beginning of an answer."

I braced myself, holding Lu closer. If this was the end, I would face it with her in my arms.

Lorde whined, sensing our tension. She limped back to us and sat on the other side of Lu, leaning hard against her.

"Lula," Cupid said, "for some reason, you decided Jo and Calvin should find each other." He wasn't waiting for an answer, so neither of us spoke.

"You did everything you could to make sure they spoke, *connected*. When they nearly ended that connection, you brought them back together, asked them to speak and find truth. That very much interests me, you doing my job."

Lu squeezed my side, bracing herself. "I didn't do anything more than an online dating site would have done."

He smiled. It was wicked and pure. "Oh, I know exactly what you did. And if they are together, even for a little time...." His voice drifted off and his eyes flashed with galaxies—endless darkness, bolts of light—all in a moment, all gone too soon.

Dangerous, this god. Powerful. But also melancholy. Hopeful.

"What you've done, Lula," he said, "is good. I'm impressed with your instincts and your skill. What I'm asking you—you and Brogan—are three things.

"One: you work for me, bringing people together who belong together. Two: you find a few things I want. Three: you deliver a few items for me."

It was a lot. It was too much. Foolish, so foolish to tie ourselves to a god.

I opened my mouth to say no, but before I could, Lu spoke over me.

"For what? What do we get if we agree? If we do all that for you?"

"Three things." He held up two fingers and his thumb. "I mend Lorde's leg. Good as new." His middle finger bent down. "I help you find that book you're carrying the key to." Pointer finger dropped. "And I keep you this way, both of you solid, in this world, alive —well, as much as you have been—able to see each other, hear each other, touch each other."

Lu sucked in a gasp and held that breath.

It was more than we could have hoped for. It was everything, this deal offered on the side of a rough and broken road. I should take it without question.

But I was made to question.

"We need more than that," I said. "Some assurance we're not just pawns you want to push around. We are in a position of weakness in this negotiation. We refuse to deal with gods when there's no skin in the game for the deity."

Bo's eyebrows shot up, sending wrinkles over his forehead. "You've bargained with gods before, have you?"

"Once."

"Which god?" he asked, "No, I can see. It was Mithra, wasn't it?"

Neither of us spoke.

"I see I haven't given you reason to trust me, especially if Mithra is all you have to go on. So how about I put some skin in the game? What would you ask from me?"

It was tempting, so tempting to ask for the monster who had done this to us. To have it sniveling at our feet, to have the thing—whatever weapon or spell that might be—to kill it. To pull that trigger, to recite those words.

I looked at Lu. Her gaze was steady. The need for revenge was there, as clearly as if it were my own. She nodded.

"We want a way to break the deal with you," I said, and Lu's eyes went wide. "We want your protection and will do what you ask of us for the benefits you have offered, but we want a way to break the agreement and walk away at any moment, at our discretion, with absolutely no repercussions from you."

Lu nodded slightly. This would give us more than the monster. Our chances of surviving once we got our hands on it were fifty-fifty. We might kill it, it might kill us. There was no telling what would happen after that. Would Lu and I remain unalive and together, but apart? Would our souls return to our own bodies? Would we die?

No, this deal, this condition with this god, gave us something better than revenge.

It gave us time.

Together. Always.

"You asked for two things, Brogan Gauge," Bo said. "My protection and a way to break the agreement."

"Those are our terms," Lula said.

In that moment, I couldn't have been prouder to be her husband.

The god studied us. I could not read his expression.

"All right," he said, slowly, as if he were about to take a shot of a drink he'd never tried before. His boots crunched in the dirt and gravel as he crossed the short distance to us. He held out his right hand, GOLD tattooed across the knuckles, the dove shifting in flight, feathers liquid silver and melted sunlight.

"You have my word."

Just that—his agreement—rolled through me like an earthquake.

Lu and I both reached out at the same time, my palm against the back of her hand, our fingers slotted.

Together.

"You have my word," Lu said.

"And mine," I added. My heart was beating fast— too fast. If we did this, everything would change.

But if we didn't…nothing would change.

Our flesh touched his, and he felt warm, human, but with something more, something like sunlit laughter and moonlight dreams right there in our hands.

Something like love.

"Oh," I said, as Lu exhaled a soft sound.

"Good." Bo grasped our hands, firm and real and kind. "This is good. I'm already pleased. With the deal. With the two of you."

Lorde lifted her head and bopped her nose on our still-grasped hands.

Bo chuckled. "The three of you. I wouldn't forget you, Lorde. You're a part of this. Of them. Of us."

And when he looked into my eyes, such relief rushed through me, cool water, a river endless with life, filling the dry, hopeless canyon of my mind, my heart. He was a breeze softly blowing, the soothing brush of a hand on skin fevered and stinging.

Then. Right then. Just to feel alive again. Just to feel Lu again. Just to know we were not alone. It was more than I'd hoped for.

My throat tightened as I choked back a sob. Tears prickled at the edges of my eyes. I exhaled, shaky, grateful.

Relief. Solace. Succor.

Lu leaned her head into my shoulder, blinking back tears.

The comfort of his presence flowed over us, holding, soothing, keeping. Neither of us wanted to let go of his hand, held now safe, finally safe in his protection.

"I think," Bo said, as the world went on around us, buzzing and busy and beautiful, "this might be the beginning of something unforgettable."

"Magic," Lu said.

"Better than that," he promised, and I could tell he meant it, could feel the ties between us and him strengthening with every passing moment, every beat of my heart.

"Now it's time to begin." He stepped back, his fingers dragging across ours before he let go, and knelt in front of Lorde again. "Let's start with your leg, sweet girl. After that, there's a book I need you to find." He glanced up at us. "You might have seen it recently buried beneath a broken shack."

Lu's free hand—the one not clasped with mine, because she could not let go, I could not let go if I tried —drifted up to the feather key hanging on the chain with the watch.

"That's the one." Bo wrapped his hand around Lorde's leg. The power that rolled through him, through us, was a zing of sound and color and *gold, gold, gold.*

"I might have a town you should go to, a rabbit you should find. Well, as much a rabbit as anything else. You'll know her when you see her." He petted Lorde's head again, running his fingers up her ears.

Then he stood and planted his fists on his hips. "How's that sound?"

Lorde walked over to us, tail wagging, her black tongue happy. No limp. Not even a slight hesitation in her gait.

I nodded, squeezing Lu's hand as she scrubbed Lorde's fuzzy head. "That sounds like a good start."

And it was.

EPILOGUE

L u wanted me.

It was in the sparkle of her eyes as she walked backward from the truck door, the keys dangling on one finger in front of her, as if those keys were what drew me to her, as if that truck, that ridiculous silver pile of junk, was what I wanted.

"I'll let you drive," she crooned as she ran one hand along the length of the truck, pausing to cup the fuel cap before dragging her full palm against the long bed.

"Damn right, I'll drive," I growled.

Back, back, back, she walked, slowly, as if hypnotized. Her pupils were already blown, her breathing fast.

I was in no better shape, breathing too hard, heart pumping like an engine, sweat—actual sweat—prickling at the back of my neck, at my temples, cooling under the lick of a breeze.

I followed her, step-for-step, as if we were built in the

rhythm of each other, as if we were locked into the metronome *tick, tick, tick* of fate, of love.

"You like the truck," she teased, her fingers dancing across the corner of the tailgate. "You might even love it a little."

"Not even a little," I said, closing the distance, easing closer to her, so close she had to press her shoulder blades to the tailgate and lean back.

We were not touching, not yet.

The ache, the torture of it, burned sublime.

We'd watched the god ride away on his motorcycle. Stared after him as he faded in the distance, moving north, down Route 66.

The ties between us were there, but less noticeable, the intensity of the connection easing.

We couldn't hear his thoughts, feel his emotions, or sense his power around us.

If not for Lorde's healed leg and my return to physicality, it might have been as if the god of connections and destruction had never waited for us on a dirt pullout north of Lawndale, the Kickapoo Creek slinking quiet and green beneath the Mother Road.

Since the god had driven north, Lu turned the truck south, one hand locked on top of mine resting upon her thigh.

We didn't speak.

We didn't turn on the radio.

We drove. Lincoln, Broadwell, Elkhart, Williamsville, Sherman. The rumble of the truck beneath us, Lorde sticking her head out the passenger window to warm her face in the sun and sniff the summer breeze.

Lu turned the truck down a road gone to grass and weeds, bright yellow coneflowers on either side of the lane, random as tossed confetti. The brush grew taller. White oak and ash trees gave glimpses of sky between branches as they lined then crowded the road.

We'd been here by the Sangamon River before, Lu and I. This little forgotten turnoff hidden in the parkland where old trees offered shade and the drone and click of insects flickering in the tall grass was its own music.

Here, the highway was gone, all sounds of the modern world swallowed up.

"Since you don't like this truck," Lu said, as I pinned her in place by locking my arms on either side of her shoulders, "not even a little, I'm thinking we'd better go find us a hotel room somewhere. Some soft bed. Shouldn't take more than an hour or two to find one not so filled with ghosts it would drive you out of your mind."

I growled, the sound primal and deep in my chest.

She ducked and spun, escaping my arms, making a dash for the driver's door, her laughter lifting bright and high.

She didn't get three steps before I caught her, my arms around her waist. She lunged, and I lifted, bringing her just off her feet as I pulled her back, until she was pressed fully against me.

"No hotels," I rumbled against the side of her neck.

"But the truck is—"

"Fine. The truck is fine. And it's going to be even better when you're in it." I lifted her again, up to her tiptoes. She made a soft sound that sent a shiver through me as she relaxed and molded her body against mine.

Her hands fell on my arms, tapping, asking, squeezing, and I released my hold.

She spun and draped her arms around my neck. "Promises, promises."

"I am a man of my word, Mrs. Gauge."

I bent until my forehead was resting against hers. "I love you."

"I love you," she said. "And if you don't get in the back of that truck right this second, I am going to drag you there."

I huffed out a laugh, my fingers sliding down into the back pockets of her jeans. "I was trying to take it slow."

"Don't need slow. Don't want slow. I want you. Now. So get your fine ass up into that truck, and be a man of your word, Mr. Gauge."

I pulled my hands out of her pockets, planted my palms on her hips, and guided her back to the tailgate. She pulled the latch and opened it. I absently noted the beautiful strips of dark wood planks held in place by low-set metal dividers that made up the truck bed before I scooped Lu up off her feet.

She gave a short shriek that fell into bubbling laughter.

"What are you doing?" she asked, still giggling.

"Never got to do this on our wedding night," I murmured. Because we hadn't had a wedding night. Not one recognized by churches or law.

It took some strength, but I am a big man. I got one

knee up on the tailgate, shifted my grip so I could free one hand for the side, and carried Lula up over the threshold of that old Chevy C10.

Her laughter had stopped. Now the only sound was her breath, a little halting, and the creak of the old springs as the truck took our weight.

"Lu?" I said, the hitches in her breathing worrying me. I stopped on my knees, there at the end of the bed, and gently lowered her down in my arms. "Are you all right, love?"

The tears on her face were a surprise, but the smile even more so. "You damn romantic. Look what you made me do." She sniffed hard, then wriggled one hand free and scrubbed at her eyes and cheeks.

Her face was splotchy, nose rubbed red.

She was the most beautiful thing in the universe.

"I got you," I said, "and I'm never letting you go, no matter what we have to face. We face it together."

She nodded and took one full breath before letting it out. "Brogan?"

"Yes, love?"

"I can hear your heartbeat."

And oh, how she smiled.

"Is that so? What is it saying?"

"You want to kiss me."

"Oh, I'm going to kiss you until you forget every other kiss in your life." I lowered her to the smooth truck bed, the dappling of sunlight through leaves painting her in a mosaic of light and shadow, her hair a slash of plaited red falling over her shoulder.

I paused there above her, savoring the smell of

honey and roses on her skin, the wonder of her soft smile. Sunlight edged her eyelashes in copper as she raised one eyebrow.

"Well?" she asked, reaching for me, catching at my hips and dragging fingertips down my thighs, then back up again. "What are you waiting for? Do you think we have all the time in the world?"

"Yes," I said, my whole heart and soul filling that one word. "I think we do."

UPCOMING

Need more Souls of the Road? Look for Brogan and Lula's next adventure in book 2: WAYWARD MOON

ABOUT THE AUTHOR

DEVON MONK is a national bestselling writer of urban fantasy. Her series include Ordinary Magic, Souls of the Road, West Hell Magic, House Immortal, Allie Beckstrom, and Broken Magic. She also writes the Age of Steam steampunk series, and the occasional short story which can be found in her collection: A Cup of Normal, and in various anthologies.

She has one husband, two sons, and lives in lovely, rainy Oregon. When not writing, Devon is drinking too much coffee, watching hockey, or knitting silly things.

Want to read more from Devon?

Follow her blog, or sign up for her newsletter, at www.devonmonk.com

ALSO BY DEVON MONK

ORDINARY MAGIC

Death and Relaxation

Devils and Details

Gods and Ends

Rock Paper Scissors

Dime a Demon

Hell's Spells

Sealed with a Tryst

At Death's Door

WEST HELL MAGIC

Hazard

Spark

HOUSE IMMORTAL

House Immortal

Infinity Bell

Crucible Zero

SHORT STORIES

A Cup of Normal (collection)

Yarrow, Sturdy and Bright (Once Upon a Curse anthology)

A Small Magic (Once Upon a Kiss anthology)

Little Flame (Once Upon a Ghost anthology)